STROKING MIDNIGHT

Michele Drake Haddad

13HORROR.COM BOOKS
An imprint of
DIZZY EMU PUBLISHING
1714 N McCadden Place, Hollywood, Los Angeles 90028
dizzyemupublishing.com

Stroking Midnight
Michele Drake Haddad

First published in the United States
in 2022 by 13Horror.com Books/Dizzy Emu Publishing

STROKING MIDNIGHT

Michele Drake Haddad

STROKING MIDNIGHT

Written by

Michele Drake Haddad

Inspired by (somewhat) real events.

NOTHING SUCCEEDS LIKE EXCESS....

                                        UNDER BLACK:

Sounds of HEAVY BREATHING.

                                        FADE IN:

Light filters in as a hand THUDS against a wall, barely
discernible, our POV travels down arm, flashes at a breast
smooshed up against the wall, SEXUAL GRUNTING ensues, the arm
pushes away to achieve better support while lower body is
subjected to rapid THRUSTS from behind.

We now make out the thigh of a leg, bent at knee, then up to
the-

                                        SMASH CUT TO:

INT. HOLMBY HILLS MANSION - NEW YEARS EVE 1928 - NIGHT

The Great Hall chandelier exudes a warm candlelight glow.
French doors and windows encompass the two story room
decorated with New Year's Eve party streamers. An up-scale
Black tie affair packed with GUESTS.

Alcohol flows freely, so does the upper-crust BANTER as Mrs.
AMANDA Letts, 20s, a raven haired young woman, appears on the
second floor at the dual staircase apex. She catches her
breath, smooths over beautiful white chiffon Channel gown
with flowing high-low hemline.

AMANDA descends the staircase, re-adjusts the hair-pin in her
chignon bun worn very low at the back of her neck, scans the
sea of faces, joins TWO WOMEN. WOMAN #1, 30s, sips a gin fizz
and drills WOMAN #2, 40s.

                    WOMAN #1
          To what school was your daughter
          was accepted?

                    WOMAN #2
          Westlake School for girls.

                    AMANDA
          Westlake? Oh yes! The school that
          moved to Holmby Hills this year.

AMANDA ignores MR. LETTS, 30's, and his possessive glare, as
he trots down staircase. AMANDA moves through the CROWD,
spots the chairperson of the Botanical Society, GRETA at the
hors d'oeuvre table, she joins her.

                    GRETA
          Such a beautiful dress Amanda.

                    AMANDA
          Thank you Greta, I'd like to
          introduce you to my Aunt Tilde,
          she's in town from Boston and is
          interested in becoming a donor.

AT THE VERANDA BAR

A beautiful black woman, DARLA, 20s, speaks with LETTS.

                    DARLA
          I appreciate your invitation.

LETTS observes AMANDA from beyond the leaded glass french
doors as he speaks.

                    MR. LETTS
          I look forward to introducing you
          to my wife.

LETTS lights cigar, PUFFS.

AMANDA guides GRETA toward the veranda bar where AUNT TILDE,
50s, nurses bourbon on the rocks.

                    AUNT TILDE
                (obnoxious)
          Where were you? The guests surely
          expect to see you by your husband's
          side.

                    AMANDA
          I needed to use the lavatory.

                    GRETA
          Who is that woman with your
          husband? Her jet black short wavy
          bob is to die for!

AMANDA and AUNT TILDE follow GRETA's gaze.

                    AUNT TILDE
                (tipsy slur)
          How brave of her. Why don't you cut
          your hair Amanda, you'd look
          cute...Amanda?

AMANDA is stunned, then forces the look of shock -- both she
and DARLA share for a brief moment -- off her face when LETTS
signals AMANDA to join them. Instead, AMANDA looks away and
slips her arm around AUNT TILDE's shoulder.

                    AMANDA
               (nervous)
          Aunt Tilde you know I prefer it
          long. How about some coffee?

                    LETTS
               (above the crowd noise)
          Amanda darling, over here!

                    AMANDA
          Excuse me ladies.

                    LETTS
               (as Amanda joins him)
          How kind of you to acquiesce. I
          would like to introduce you to
          someone.

DARLA offers her hand along with a poker-face.

                    DARLA
          DARLA.

                    LETTS
          We are doing some business
          together.

                    AMANDA
          Amanda. How do you do? What type of
          business?

                    DARLA
          Real Estate.

                    AMANDA
          Well, you certainly have come to
          the right party. Ownership is on
          the tip of everyone's tongue
          tonight.

MR. PARK, 30's, holding a camera, taps AMANDA's shoulder. She
spins around.

                    AMANDA (CONT'D)
          Mr. Park. Great to see you here.

                    MR. PARK
          The pleasure is all mine. I told
          you, call me Jack.
               (MORE)

                    MR. PARK (CONT'D)
                  (to Letts)
          How about a photo?

                    LETTS
          Perfect. You too Darla!

LETTS positions DARLA next to AMANDA.

                    AMANDA
                  (to Letts)
          What about you?

                    LETTS
          I need to check on the band.

MR. PARK's camera bulb FLASHES.

A passing BUTLER offers Darla a glass of champagne, she
shakes her head no.

A JUGGLER tosses celebratory silver balls in the air that
JINGLE. A PARTY GUEST whispers in AMANDA's ear. DARLA backs
away into the crowd.

INT. MANSION KITCHEN - NIGHT - CONTINUOUS

AMANDA enters, finds LETTS alone. With his back to her, he
finishes pouring from a MAGNUM OF CRISTAL.

                    AMANDA
          Congratulations, it's a great
          party. You outdid yourself once
          again.

LETTS spins on his black cap-toed oxfords, holds two CRYSTAL
ART DECO FLUTES of champagne.

                    LETTS
          Look familiar?

                    AMANDA
          Our wedding flutes, how sweet.

No response save a sheepish grin. He offers AMANDA a glass.
She doesn't accept.

                    AMANDA (CONT'D)
          It's almost midnight, shouldn't we
          have our toast in the great hall?

                    LETTS
          I wanted you to myself.

LETTS deposits flutes on counter, grabs AMANDA close, with a
knowing look of obedience she rotates in his arms, braces
herself.

With AMANDA's back to him, LETTS tears up.

                    LETTS (CONT'D)
          Relax. Let's drink.

AMANDA lets out a deep sigh, turns toward LETTS, accepts the
champagne.

                    LETTS (CONT'D)
               (smiles)
          Cheers!

Glasses clink. They both down their bubbly. AMANDA HICCUPS.

                    AMANDA
          A little sweet for Cristal, don't
          you think?

AMANDA's pupils quickly dilate.

                    LETTS
          I added something extra special in
          your glass. To celebrate.

LETTS retrieves a small vial from his inner suit pocket,
takes a hearty sniff.

                    AMANDA
          Oh goody!

                    LETTS
          Let us celebrate our confessions
          and proclaim our New Year's
          resolutions!

                    AMANDA
               (suddenly woozy)
          What did you do?

AMANDA's HEART POUNDS, she catches a difficult breath. She
COUGHS, struggling to lift up her glass.

                    AMANDA (CONT'D)
               (hoarse whisper)
          Water.

WHAP! LETTS slaps AMANDA, knocking the empty crystal
champagne glass to the floor, it SHATTERS. An unspoken volume
of tension builds between the couple as a red welt swells up
on AMANDA's ivory face. A single tear rolls down her cheek.

                    LETTS
                  (snarls)
         How dare you humiliate me. You are
         a disgrace to the family!

Horrified, AMANDA rushes out.

INT. MANSION GREAT HALL - NIGHT

Seeing double, AMANDA stops, teeters, GAGS.

The Great Hall filled with GUESTS, appears hazy. Their
LAUGHTER WANES as peripheral sound is lost to the BUZZ in
AMANDA's head, she makes her way toward DARLA.

                    AMANDA
         He knows, Oh God, he Knows!

But no one can hear her. The CROWD CHANTS a celebratory
countdown to midnight.

                    CROWD
                  (in unison)

TEN! NINE! EIGHT!

We see the horror on DARLA's face as blood trickles down
AMANDA's nose, and out of her eyes.

AMANDA spits out blood, sucks in a RASPY WHEEZE.

                    CROWD
            SEVEN! SIX! FIVE! FOUR!

AMANDA strains to reach out to DARLA with a horrific
realization she is paralyzed, mouth wide open, unable to
breathe.

                    CROWD (CONT'D)
              THREE! TWO!-

AMANDA falls backward to marble floor, SPLAT!

SCREAMS from the GUESTS, DARLA drops to her knees next to
AMANDA.

Sprawled, face up, bright red blood oozes from back of
AMANDA's head into a large crimson puddle. LOUD HEARTBEAT
SOUNDS as one of the juggler's silver balls rolls into the
BLOOD PUDDLE.

A final, feeble WHEEZE escapes AMANDA's blood foamed mouth, HEARTBEAT SOUND stops.

                    DARLA
          NO!!!!!!!!

                                        CUT TO BLACK

HAUNTINGLY TRAGIC MUSIC UNDER as the words "Stroking Midnight" FILTER INTO VIEW.

                                   UNDER BLACK:

Sounds of HEAVY BREATHING.

CHYRON: FIFTY YEARS LATER

                                        FADE IN:

Light filters in as a hand THUDS against a wall, barely discernible, our POV travels down arm, flashes at a breast smooshed up against the wall, SEXUAL GRUNTING ensues, the arm pushes away to achieve better support while lower body is subjected to rapid THRUSTS from behind.

We now make out the thigh of a leg, bent at knee, then up to the-

                                   SMASH CUT TO:

INT. ART DECO STUDIO APT. (1978) - MORNING

A young black woman GASPS as she springs up from the waist in bed, LILY JACKSON, 20s, the spitting image of her grandmother Darla, except for the hair.

LILY's brow is wet with sweat. From LILY's expression, we gather this is a reoccurring nightmare. She pulls mini journal from robe pocket, we witness LILY jotting down a few notes.

I had the dream again, identities still not discernible.

LILY reacts as if she senses someone else is also in the room with her. She scans her surroundings.

Original Art Deco plaster, Cornish moulding, frame the petite room with timeless elegance from above. An antique desk, dresser with vanity mirror, and a quaint table and two chairs are the only sizable furnishings.

A wall sconce light fixture beams a halo over table where a single cup and saucer reside on one placemat, LILY's day-calendar, pager, and extra-long corded princess telephone on the other.

A small fridge is tucked into original ice-box space, an iron, hot plate, and toaster, sit on counter underneath single cupboard.

LILY's attention settles above the front door on an antique wall clock that hangs vicariously by a thin metal wire. Clock reads 10 o'clock.

LILY jumps off and lifts Murphy bed by handle, tucks it into wall.

EXT. WESTWOOD APARTMENT BUILDING - DAY

At the foot of the stairs. LILY speaks with apartment manager JACK, now an elderly man who wears thick bifocals and vintage flat cap.

LILY offers him a faint smile, and a check. JACK studies it.

                    LILY
          I'm sorry it's a little light. I'll
          get you the rest next week.
                    (on Jack's look of
                    concern)
          You must have rented 1A, though, I
          hear tapping on the walls.

LILY recalls the sounds, TAP! TAP! Inciting,

                    FLASHES OF MEMORY
          LILY brushing her teeth in front of
          mirrored medicine cabinet, her
          reflection suddenly blurry with
          movement in sync with loud TAP!
          TAP! TAP from wall behind it.

LILY lies in bed, it shakes in sync with TAP! TAP from wall behind her.

AND BACK!

                    JACK
          No. It's still vacant.

                    LILY
          Oh.

LILY at a loss for words as JACK closes door.

INT. ACTOR'S STUDIO - NIGHT

LILY is on stage with fellow ACTOR. ACTOR goes to kiss her,
she flinches, he whispers in her ear, she pulls away, then
escapes from ACTOR's embrace. ACTING COACH critiques
ominously from somewhere in the room.

                    ACTING COACH
          No, no, no, no. LILY! You have got
          to stop anticipating! What did you
          glean from your dream assignment?
          Use that pretty head of yours to
          think!

LILY and ACTOR stare straight ahead toward ACTING STUDENTS
who sit before them in darkened audience bleachers.

                    LILY
          But when I think, I anticipate.

ACTING STUDENTS LAUGH.

                    ACTOR
          It was my fault. I fed her the
          wrong cue at the wrong time.

                    ACTING COACH
          How noble of you. As actors, we
          must remember to tap into our
          creative spirit! We can find
          strength in embracing our dark
          side, holding still, allowing our
          feelings to emote in a natural
          rhythm.

                    LILY
          I though you wanted me to be
          dramatic.

                    ACTING COACH
          Stop Lily. Listen to the note
          behind the note. Swallow your
          pride, open your heart. I can't
          help you leave this place with more
          than you are open to receive.

LILY wipes a tear, stands tall.

                         ACTING COACH (CONT'D)
               This is important class, outward
               appearances alone won't get us what
               we need in life or on the stage.
                    (beat)
               What's it gonna be Lily? Are you
               willing to face your inner demons?
                    (on Lily's nod)
               Great! Next scene! Bill and Thomas
               you're up next.

INT. PHONE BOOTH - NIGHT

Frustrated, LILY dials zero on the pay phone base. RED LIGHT
pulses through glass upon LILY's face, creates grotesque
shadows. Paranoid, she maintains astute surveillance of her
surroundings while she speaks.

                         LILY
                    (into phone)
               Hello operator, I'd like to make a
               collect call.

EXT. DARLA'S HOME - BIRMINGHAM ALABAMA - NIGHT - CONTINUOUS

Under the moonlight, DARLA, 79, weathered looking and gray,
rocks in a white wooden chair on front porch. Phone RINGS
from inside the house, prompts DARLA to abandon her reverie.
It takes some effort for her to shuffle toward the front door
with a diabetic-impaired gait. The porch-light CLICKS on.

                         DARLA
                    (out-loud)
               I'm coming, I'm coming!

INTERCUT - DARLA'S KITCHEN/LILY'S PAYPHONE - NIGHT

RING! DARLA flips wall switch, RING! Grabs receiver from
phone base mounted on wall underneath a large green and white
Atropa belladonna poster. It is obvious from the kitchen's
contents, Darla is a herbalist.

                         DARLA
                    (into phone)
               Of course I'll accept.

                         LILY
                    (into phone)
               Grandma? It's me.

We hear DARLA COUGHING through LILY's phone receiver.

                    LILY (CONT'D)
               (into phone)
          See, you do need me!

                    DARLA
               (into phone)
          Girl, I need my rest, do you know
          what time it is here?

                    LILY
               (into phone)
          What's that herb mix you use to
          help with sleep issues?

                    DARLA
               (into phone)
          What's wrong darlin?

LILY cries.

                    DARLA (CONT'D)
               (into phone)
          Tell me child. Kendel says you
          don't call him any more.

Lily spaces out. We see snippets of Lily's earlier nightmare
inside her head.

                    DARLA (CONT'D)
               (into phone)
          Lily?

                    LILY
               (into phone)
          It's just that, everywhere I go,
          everything I do...I draw the wrong
          kind of attention, there's no
          escape. I'm having nightmares-

                    DARLA
               (into phone)
          -Stay strong LILY! Have you been
          saying your prayers?

                    LILY
               (into phone)
          Not enough I suppose.
               (wipes away tear)
          Plus, I suck at acting.

                    DARLA
               (into phone)
          Well, now that's not true.
               (MORE)

                    DARLA (CONT'D)
          You sure put on a good act to get
          outta the house when your momma was
          dying!

Dead silence.

                    DARLA (CONT'D)
               (into phone)
          I'm sorry.

                    LILY
               (into phone)
          No, I deserved that. Anyway, it
          costs money to make money, my phone
          was cut off last week, I'm always
          short on rent and I think Kendel
          must be here in Los Angeles.

                    DARLA
               (into phone, serious)
          He is in jail, Lily. Now stop this
          nonsense and get some sleep. And
          don't you give up! We'll talk more
          another time.

DARLA hangs up phone receiver.

It CLICKS in LILY's ear.

EXT. STREET - NIGHT

LILY exits phone booth, knits her brows, scans surroundings,
takes a deep breath.

She cringes as she passes PEEP SHOW VENUE with lurid posters
under the RED LIGHTS. She dusts off unwanted stares from a
few SEEDY CLIENTELE.

The corner streetlight FLICKERS.

                                        MATCH CUT TO:

EXT. LILY'S APARTMENT BUILDING - NIGHT - CONTINUOUS

Streetlight FLICKERS, LILY still on foot, comes in to view,
approaches building. A few small landscape lanterns offer
minimal light for LILY's stroll among the shadows. SNAP!
Something moves in bushes near apartment stairwell.

From LILY's POV we see a SHADOWY FIGURE move on second floor.
LILY finds rock in foliage underneath Streetlight's FAINT
BEAM, prays.

                    LILY
               (under her breath)
          Though I walk through the valley of
          the shadow of death, I will fear no
          evil, for you are with me, your rod
          and your staff comfort me.

INT. ART DECO APARTMENT - NIGHT

It's dark. LILY enters, closes door behind her, CLICKS three
deadbolt locks closed, moves toward wall sconce light switch,
FLICKS. FLICKS again. It doesn't work. Sudden sound of
RUNNING TAP WATER from adjoined bathroom.

                    LILY
               Who's there?!

MATCH STRIKES, LILY lights up bathroom door handle, it moves,
LILY covers her mouth in terror with free hand.

                    LILY (CONT'D)
               I'm calling the police!

LILY picks up receiver. Of course, no dial tone! Match goes
out.

                    DARKNESS
          The loud TICK TOCK, TICK TOCK from
          wall clock competes with LILY's
          POUNDING HEARTBEAT.

                    LILY
               If you want money, you're out of
               luck, I'm officially flat broke.

LILY rushes to front door, scrambles to unlatch deadbolts,
the last one is jammed.

Bathroom door CREAKS open.

Scared shitless, LILY turns around with back to front door,
drops the rock. From an unknown point of view we see the
terror on LILY's face, she picks up rock, swirls around,
pounds the jammed deadbolt.

WHAP! Wall clock above door jam plummets LILY's HEAD, she
hits floor with a THUD.

EXT. WESTWOOD APARTMENT BUILDING - NIGHT - LATER

At the foot of the stairs. JACK opens his front door. DOGS
BARKING.

                         JACK
             Jesus. What happened to you?

LILY's face is covered in blood.

                         LILY
             May I use your phone?

EXT/INT. ART DECO STUDIO APT. - NIGHT

On the top floor, LILY, bandaid at her hairline, waits with
bated breath outside her open apartment door.

MOTORCYCLE COP, CORY, 30s, struts up the stairs toward her.
He's awfully good looking.

Inside apartment, CORY checks out LILY's space by flashlight.

                         CORY
             Nothing out of the ordinary here
             that I can see Miss-

                         LILY
             -Lily. Lily Jackson.

CORY turns to LILY, gives her a once over. LILY squirms.

CORY flips through LILY's day calendar, picks up a photo.

                         COPY CORY
             You're a model?

                         LILY
             Actress.

                         CORY
             I see. Another lonely gal looking
             for some attention.

                         LILY
             Oh no sir, I swear to you someone-

                         CORY
             -No I get it.

CORY snatches what looks like a business card tucked in
dresser mirror.

                         CORY (CONT'D)
             You best be careful then, walking
             alone at night.

                    LILY
          I don't think I mentioned that.

CORY stuffs card in leather jacket pocket.

                    CORY
               (shrugs)
          For evidence.

LILY's freezes as CORY lifts her chin.

                    CORY (CONT'D)
          You're not on drugs are you?

                    LILY
          Oh no sir, I-

CORY's walkie talkie BUZZES. He holds up hand to silence her
to hear walkie talkie POLICE CHATTER.

                    CORY
               (as he exits)
          You should have your landlord fix
          the pipes. You'd be surprised how
          much havoc old buildings can cause
          the soul.

LILY shuts door, locks all bolts. She moves to window, the
lurid RED LIGHTS from across the street pulse, causing eerie
shadows to flit across her apartment walls. LILY draws shade
closed.

INT. SMALL PRODUCTION OFFICE - HOLLYWOOD, CALIFORNIA - DAY

IN THE WAITING ROOM

LILY is surrounded by a gaggle of ACTORS, and walls covered
with Paradise lost, by Clifford Odets posters. LILY adjusts
her straight-hair-wig-with-bangs, as she waits her turn. A
CASTING ASSISTANT enters.

                    CASTING ASSISTANT
          Ms. Jackson.

IN THE MEETING ROOM

LILY in the throes of her audition.

                         LILY
                    (sweet)
               "No, there is more to life than
               this...That was the past, but there
               is a future."

FIVE INDEPENDENT FILM EXECS give LILY a snarky once over then
huddle. After what seems like a lifetime,

                         EXEC
               Can you loose the angelic glow?

LILY holds finger up to symbolize one minute, faces corner
away from group, takes a moment to prepare, circles back,
faces EXECS.

                         LILY
                    (serious)
               "No, there is more to life than
               this...That was the past, but there
               is a future."

A single, slow methodical CLAP. LILY boughs.

                         EXEC
                    (flat)
               We'll be in touch.

                         LILY
                    (heartbroken)
               I can do it again if you'd like.

EXT. HOLLYWOOD BLVD. - DAY

With furrowed brow, LILY dodges daily parade of colorful
souls on her way to bus stop. An exceptionally large crowd of
LOCALS and TOURISTS are in process of boarding.

BUS takes off, LILY and a few OTHERS, are left to vie for
other transportation options.

                         LILY
                    (out-loud)
               Shoot!

MOTORCYCLE COP pulls up to curb, takes off helmet.

                         CORY
               Hello beautiful.

LILY ignores him.

                    COP CORY
          Looks like you're in need of a
          ride. I'm off duty now, how about a
          cup of coffee?

                    LILY
          No thank you.

LILY waves down CHECKER CAB.

CHECKER CAB pulls up in front of Cop's motorcycle.

EXT./INT. CHECKER CAB - DAY

The back passenger door is locked. LILY peers in the window,
The back seat is full of luggage. CAB DRIVER, leans over
front bench seat unlocks door with a CLICK. Hesitant, LILY
opens front passenger door.

                    CAB DRIVER
               (smiles)
          You can sit up here if you like.
          I'm delivering some lost luggage
          from the Airport.

                    LILY
          Thanks anyway, I'm late for work as
          it is.

COP REVS MOTORCYCLE ENGINE.

                    CAB DRIVER
          Not to worry. They've waited this
          long for the luggage, where you
          headed?

                    LILY
          Beverly Drive?

CAB DRIVER pats seat. LILY darts a nervous look back at COP.

                    LILY (CONT'D)
          Okay, I really appreciate it.

INT. NATE'N AL'S DELICATESSEN RESTAURANT - DAY

LILY expertly balances five plates and delivers them safely
to a booth of LUNCH PATRONS.

LUNCH PATRON #1

Wow, that's what I call talent!

                    LILY
          So far it's my only claim to fame.

LUNCH PATRON #2

Don't be so hard on yourself sweetheart.

LILY notices BIBLE on TABLE, smiles. LUNCH PATRON #3, removes
slip of paper from BIBLE.

LUNCH PATRON #3

Here. I've seen you in my acting class.

                    LILY
          What is it?

LUNCH PATRON #3

An Open Call for a parody of Noah's Ark.

LUNCH PATRON #2

He means Cattle Call.

EVERYONE LAUGHS but LILY .

A PAGER BUZZES. EVERYONE at the table checks their pagers.
LILY wipes her hands on 3-pocket apron, checks her pager,
checks the room, DELI MANAGER glares at LILY from across the
deli case, shakes head no.

LILY's PAGER BUZZES again, she ignores.

                    LILY
          Can I get you anything else?

LILY deposits check on table before they can answer.

IN THE HALLWAY

LILY checks her pager. Battery is dead.

EMPLOYEE LOCKER AREA - LATER

LILY closes her locker. Another waitress, MIRANDA, 30s, rolls
a wad of dollar bills, stuffs in LILY's back pocket.

                    MIRANDA
          Your share of the tips.

MIRANDA lights cigarette, offers LILY one, retracts the
offer.

                    MIRANDA (CONT'D)
          I forgot, you don't smoke.

Blows smoke away from LILY.

                    MIRANDA (CONT'D)
          Sorry. You need a ride home today?

LILY parks her bum on bench, props her head in hands, with
elbows to knees.

                    LILY
          I need my own wheels. But I can't
          afford it.

                    MIRANDA
          Look, I told you how you can make
          some extra money. Knowing you, you
          threw away the card. I think I have
          another one here somewhere.

Miranda digs in her purse with one hand, tags another drag
off cigarette with the other.

                    MIRANDA (CONT'D)
          Do you think I support two kids by
          waiting tables alone?

                    LILY
          It's okay. I'll figure something
          out.

DELI MANAGER waltzes in spraying air freshener.

                    DELI MANAGER
          Why the glum faces, it's payday!

EXT. NATE'N AL'S DELICATESSEN RESTAURANT - DAY

LILY and MIRANDA stroll toward and enter a FORD PINTO.

                    LILY
          Do you mind if we stop by Erewhon
          after the bank? I need to pick up a
          herbal remedy.

                    MIRANDA
          Sure you don't want to stop for a
          drink at Carriage trade?
                    (on Lily's look.)
          You could have a club soda.

                    LILY
          Thanks, but I gotta get my house in
          order.

INT. MIRANDA'S FORD PINTO - DAY - MOVING

                    MIRANDA
          Yours is the next block, right?

What's the matter?

LILY concentrates on passenger side car mirror. CORY'S
MOTORCYCLE moves in and out of view.

                    LILY
          I thought I recognized somebody.
          That cop I told you about.

EXT. WESTWOOD APARTMENT BUILDING - DAY

At the foot of the stairs. LILY hands JACK a check. He
studies it, smiles.

                    LILY
          Sorry it took so long. We're good,
          right?

                    JACK
          I had the pipes and Murphy bed
          latch checked today. Telephone
          company came and went. We're good.

INT. ART DECO STUDIO APT. - NIGHT

LILY enters living space from bathroom area, her head wrapped
in a bath-towel, she sports a short, salmon colored, floral
chenille robe. From Lilly's POV we something tucked in vanity
mirror.

A silhouette moves behind her.

THUD! Murphy bed unleashes itself from the wall. LILY pivots
slowly, scanning the room. Satisfied, she FLICKS off wall
sconce.

DARKNESS. RUSTLING SOUNDS as LILY settles in bed. HEAVY
BREATHING.

                    LILY
          Who's there!?

LILY jumps out of bed, SNAPS on bathroom light, leaves
bathroom door ajar, lands back on bed, sleepless.

Red light strobes through window shade, bounces on Lily's
face as the indiscernible shadowy figure looms up behind her.

EXT. BAPTIST CHURCH HOMELESS OUTREACH SOUP KITCHEN - DAY

In the small parking near a makeshift basketball hoop LILY
ladles soup into small wooden bowls for some HOMELESS FOLK. A
YOUNG KID makes a basket, then scurries into line, takes
cuts. LILY serves the YOUNG KID.

                    LILY
          I tastes better when you wait your
          turn.

                    YOUNG KID
          I was the first one here today!

                    LILY
          Great. Maybe you can help me set up
          next time.

EXT./INT. BUS - EVENING - MOVING

BUS with DESTINATION SIGN: "Westwood" creeps though traffic.

Inside, LILY observes slivers of evening sunset through bus
window in between buildings as bus edges through traffic.
Hypnotic. LILY nods off.

Bus SCREECHES to a stop. LILY's eyes pop open.

From LILY's POV we see an INTERIOR BUS CARD ADVERTISEMENT
above passenger seats that reads: "Playboy's 25th Anniversary
Great Playmate Hunt".

INT. LILY'S STUDIO APT. - NIGHT

Phone RINGING. LILY stares at the circular dial as it lights
up with each RING. She takes a dropper-full of liquid herbs
from small bottle labeled EREWHON. Finally, LILY picks up
receiver.

                    LILY
               (on phone)
          Hello?

INT. JOY YOUNG RESTAURANT - BIRMINGHAM, ALABAMA - NIGHT

At hallway's end a young black man KENDEL, 20s, wears work
apron, with phone receiver next to ear in one hand, slides
curtain closed around payphone nook for privacy with the
other. A real charmer and a repeat offender. He's obsessed
with what he can't have, and right now that something he
can't have is LILY.

INTERCUT - LILY'S APARTMENT/KENDEL'S WORK - NIGHT

                    LILY
               (into phone)
          How'd you get my number?

                    KENDEL
               (into phone)
          Darla gave it to me. Asked me to
          check up on you. See, granny and I
          are quite close, since she thinks
          we are still engaged.

                    LILY
               (into phone)
          You're in LA aren't you?

                    KENDEL
               (into phone)
          When were you going to tell her?

Too bad things aren't working out for you. I bet it is
exhausting galavanting around, pretending to be somebody
you're not.

                    LILY
               (into phone)
          I'm hanging up now!

                    KENDEL
               (into phone)
          Why? What's his name? Is he there
          now? Or is it a she!

                    LILY
               (into phone)
          Shut up!

                    KENDEL
               (into phone)
          You know I get hard when you're
          angry with me. Maybe I will come
          out to the city of angels to fuck
          the devil and all that pent up
          loneliness out of you, just like I
          used to.

                    LILY
               (into phone)
          You listen to me Kendel, I am going
          to make it here, in Los Angeles, on
          my own. I do not need your help, or
          your insults, so loose my number!

LILY BANGS phone receiver to cradle, lets out a BIG BREATH.
The wall sconce light bulb FLICKERS. The Business card is on
place-mat! LILY picks it up, we see: "Franks Figure
Photography".

INT. SKEEZY PHOTO STUDIO - DAY

This time LILY is surrounded by a gaggle of YOUNG FOLKS in
the outer office who hope to follow their Hollywood dreams
via figure modeling. LILY is the only person not wearing
spandex of some sort. Various posters decorate the wall. LILY
inspects poster of her co-worker, Miranda, we see: Miranda on
her knees, in yellow bikini bottom only, holding a drill.

A seedy looking, mustached man, FRANK, 40s, enters. The way
everyone reacts you would think he was the Messiah, except he
has a NIKON CAMERA strapped around his neck. He scans room
points to LILY.

Inside room, FRANK gestures toward small stage against a
colored backdrop. LILY obeys. The door swings closed
automatically behind them. FRANK moves toward opposite side
of room, fiddles with a toaster, it POPS UP burnt toast.

                    FRANK
          Shit.

With his back to LILY, FRANK constructs a peanut butter and
cracker sandwich. Without turning around, he speaks.

                    FRANK (CONT'D)
          What are you waiting for? Take off
          your top.

LILY gulps, painfully unbuttons her blouse. Frank is more
interested in his lunch. He turns around, wipes hands on his
jeans.

                    FRANK (CONT'D)
               (munching)
          Why so glum. I'm sure your breasts
          are beautiful.

LILY removes her blouse, FRANK removes the rest of her
clothes with his eyes.

                    LILY
          I promised myself, I wouldn't do
          this.

FRANK ignores her, SNAPS some photos, then goes back for more
peanut butter.

                    FRANK
          Would you be willing to show me
          what ya got below the waist?

LILY is mortified.

                    FRANK (CONT'D)
          For variety.

LILY's POV of FRANK's peanut butter laced mustache, magnified
as he speaks when she undresses all the way.

                    FRANK (CONT'D)
          Oh my god. Sooooo Hot!

SNAP! SNAP! LILY is creeped out, starts to dress. SNAP! SNAP!

                    FRANK (CONT'D)
               (oblivious)
          Oh, yeah, pouty is perfect, look at
          me.

SNAP!

                    FRANK
          Just a minute I need another roll
          of film.

FRANK struts over to wall cupboard, but instead, CLICKS off
the lights, except for one.

                    FRANK (CONT'D)
          It's hot in here.

Like a deer in the head lights, from the glow of a single
track-light, LILY is dressed except for blouse she holds over
her breasts.

                    FRANK (CONT'D)
          Hold it right there.

Frank crosses over to LILY, pulls her arm away from chest,
and inappropriately tweaks her nipples.

                    FRANK (CONT'D)
          Now we're talking-

LILY's face hardens like Joan of Arc burning at the stake.
FLASH!

EXT. SKEEZY PHOTO STUDIO - DAY

Despondent, LILY waits at a bus stop bench. A SMALL CHILD's
GIGGLE catches her attention. CHILD rolls by on tiny skates
while MOTHER lovingly supports her child's effort. LILY tilts
head back, faces the sky above her, a single tear rolls down
her cheek.

Sound of MOTORCYCLE ENGINE sobers her up. It's that COP. CORY
removes his helmet, waves to LILY from across the street. She
shudders, thankfully LILY's bus pulls up, blocking his sight.

INT. LILY'S STUDIO APT. - NIGHT

IN THE BATHROOM TUB

LILY is surrounded by foamy bubbles. PHONE RINGS, she takes a
breath, then submerges herself under water. PHONE RINGS a few
more times, then stops. LILY comes up for air.

IN THE LIVING AREA

Light above the small table FLICKERS.

PHONE RINGS. LILY enters from bathroom in robe, towers over
phone, doesn't answer. It RINGS several times. A long pause
after the last ring. LILY exhales deeply. Phone RINGS again,
she picks up receiver, doesn't say a word.

                    PEGGY
               (on phone filtered)
          Lily? Is this Lily Jackson's
          residence?

                    LILY
               (into phone)
          Who is this?

                    PEGGY (O.S.)
               (on phone filtered)
          This is Peggy.

                    LILY
               (into phone)
          Who?

                    PEGGY
               (on phone filtered)
          It's your agent, Peggy.

LILY cheers up.

                    LILY
               (into phone)
          Holy crap, I'm so sorry, it's been
          awhile.

                    PEGGY
               (on phone filtered)
          Well today's your lucky day, you
          know that photo shoot?

                                        CUT TO:

EXT. PLAYBOY MANSION - DAY

HOLMBY HILLS, CALIFORNIA

A LINCOLN TOWN-CAR pulls up to iron gate at 10236 Charing
Cross Road, as it closes behind a Sports car. DRIVER rolls
down window, a VOICE speaks from a ROCK positioned on the
left side of the road.

                    VOICE
               (filtered)
          Name please.

                    DRIVER
          LILY, I am dropping Lily Jackson
          off.

Iron gate slowly opens.

                    VOICE
               (filtered)
          Make sure only Ms. Jackson exits
          the vehicle, then continue driving
          out the back gate.

INT./EXT. LINCOLN TOWN-CAR - NIGHT - MOVING

LILY peers out left side passenger window up at the
magnificent rolling front lawn topped with large twin LION
STATUES.

                    LILY
          Wow!

INT. PLAYBOY MANSION / UPSTAIRS MASTER BATHROOM - NIGHT

An unknown POV witnesses elegantly pajamaed man HEF, 50s,
from the second story window arguing with a LOVELY BLONDE
WOMAN in the circular driveway. The SPORTS CAR arrives,
scoops up the woman, drives off. HEF remains, appears as if
the woman took his mojo with her. But only for a second.

BUTLER DAN enters the empty bathroom with freshly laundered
white robes. He notices the window curtains fluttering and
races over to crank the window closed.

                    BUTLER DAN
               (out-loud)
          It's colder than a witches tit in
          here!

INT. PLAYBOY MANSION / GREAT HALL - NIGHT - CONTINUOUS

LILY enters the home of Hugh Hefner, "Hef". She pauses at the
center of marble floor. The Exotic wood paneled walls glow
with light from the chandelier that hovers over the room. We
are eerily reminded this is the exact spot Amanda died fifty
years before.

INT. PLAYBOY MANSION UPSTAIRS GUEST "RED ROOM" - NIGHT

BUTLER DAN finishes folding the satin sheet-cover over the
duvet. He drops a single red rose in a bud vase that sits
next to a card as he exits.

INSERT CARD: WELCOME LILY!

                              BACK TO SCENE.

BUTLER DAN stops before a mirror, licks his finger, smoothes
his bangs. Sudden TAP! TAP! TAP! On the entry's thick wooden
door causes him to jump out of his skin.

In waltzes LILY, she tosses her carpet bag onto the bed.

                    LILY
          A room to myself?!

BUTLER DAN bows.

                    BUTLER
          They call it the Red Room.

BUTLER DAN exits. The ceiling light FLICKERS.

INT. PLAYBOY MANSION / MEDITERRANEAN ROOM - MORNING

LILY nurses a cup of coffee while a southern blonde, BETTY,
20s, wears a tell-tale white robe that announces she has
slept with Hef. She works on her bowl of grits in between
drawls.

                    BETTY
               (heavy drawl)
          I recommend the grits, it soaks up
          the previous night's alcohol. So
          how did you rate a room to
          yourself? I've been here three
          weeks and have to literally shack
          up in the barn. You must be real
          good.

                    LILY
          Excuse me? First day. There's a
          barn?

BETTY breaks into laughter.

                    BETTY
          Lets just say there are extra
          living quarters on the grounds,
          aside from the main house. Tell me,
          Did you have a visitor late last
          night?

LILY shoots a glance at BETTY.

                    BETTY (CONT'D)
          You're blushing. I knew it! He
          kicked me to the curb early.

                    LILY
          No, I would be the first to know if
          someone did, I couldn't sleep a
          wink.

                    BETTY
          Oh, your in that room.

                    LILY
          What's that supposed to mean?

BUTLER MARK enters, serves BETTY a bottle of aspirin, a glass
of water, and a look that could kill.

                    BUTLER MARK
               (to LILY)
          Don't listen to her. She's into
          crazy urban myths.

                    BETTY
          Sorry. Anyways, we best be cordial
          to each other, we may end up bunk
          mates. Whatcha in for?

                    LILY
               (nervous)
          A pictorial. Richard is the
          photographer. I hope I won't regret
          it. I keep telling myself this is
          art personified. You?

BETTY pops a few aspirin, downs with water.

                    BETTY
               (hiccups)
          I intend to be Playmate of the
          year.

                    LILY
          Good luck with that. My agent told
          me that the best way to insure I'm
          chosen for the magazine, is to
          drink Perrier and just say no to
          Hef.

EXT. PRIVATE BEACH - DAY

A magnificent cerulean sea, LILY's backdrop, glistens behind
her as she wades slowly in shallow water, she guides a
speckled white horse by the reins.

RICHARD's camera SNAPS in between his comments as LILY
strolls in a string bikini tucked smartly under an oversized
white shirt.

                    RICHARD
          That's it. Beautiful. No, don't
          look at the camera. Perfect! Now
          take off the shirt, let it drop to
          the sand. Great. Untie the bikini
          top.

LILY pauses. She's uncomfortable. Finally, she obeys.

                    RICHARD (CONT'D)
          That's it. Good. Get up on the
          horse and twist your torso toward
          me, I want the light to reflect on
          your breasts.

SNAP, SNAP, SNAP.

                    RICHARD
          Absolutely gorgeous. Eyes on the
          camera, make love to the camera.
          That's it.

From LILY's POV, a WOMAN WITH DARK FLOWING HAIR stares back
at her from off in the distance. LILY pauses, holds a free
hand to her for-head shielding her eyes from the setting sun
to discern who it is.

                    PHOTOGRAPHER
          LILY, back over here, we're loosing
          light!

The horse WHINNIES, rears on it's hind legs. The woman no
longer in sight.

INT. PLAYBOY MANSION/DINING ROOM - DAY

At the large dining table, HEF, in his usual daywear of
pajamas and smoking jacket, works along side West Coast Photo
Editor BETH, 40s as they look over LILY's horse photo slides
on a light-box.

                    HEF
          These are lovely. This photo with
          the lens flare is amazing!

From HEF's POV we see the image: LILY ON HORSEBACK, TOPLESS,
SCREENING HER EYES WITH ONE HAND OVER BROW, LOOKING OFF INTO
THE DISTANCE.

                    BETH
          She is a sweetheart with a great
          body, I think we should take
          advantage of that.

LILY enters dining room holing her carpet bag.

                    LILY
          I am surprised they turned out
          okay, I was nervous as heck. I came
          to say thank you and good-bye, time
          to get back to reality.

BETH notices HEF is transfixed with LILY.

BUTLER DAN enters.

                    BUTLER DAN
          Ms. Jackson, your CHECKERED CAB has
          arrived.

                    LILY
               (tensing up)
          I didn't call a cab.

LILY strains to catch a glimpse out the beveled glass dining
room window. It's COP CORY! He leans against Checkered Cab in
streetwear.

                    LILY (CONT'D)
          In fact that man has been stalking
          me.

                    HEF
               (to Butler Dan)
          Call security.

                    LILY
          You know, maybe I could stick
          around a little longer. Is there
          something else I could do?

                    BETH
          Actually, I have a different idea
          for your centerfold that could be
          shot here, on the grounds.

                    LILY
          Really?

Hef fills his cigar bowl, lights, PUFFS. SECURITY JOE enters.

                    HEF
          Would be happy to have you stay as
          long as you need. Joe send the cab
          away. Inform the rest of your team
          we need to tighten up a bit.

HEF rises, as his personal secretary JONI, 40s, enters and
approaches him. HEF and JONI engage in a quick, private
conversation. HEF shoots a glance at LILY.

                    JONI
          Come with me, LILY, let's get you a
          key to the guest house. The room
          upstairs will be occupied by one of
          Hef's friends for the weekend.

EXT. PLAYBOY MANSION - DAY

Beyond the circular driveway, the enormous, perfectly
manicured lawn sparkles like emeralds. The happy CHIRP of
songbirds adds to the story-book quality that permeates the
vast grounds. Surreal.

LILY chooses the stone path to the left of lawn, strolls
toward the back of mansion's West Wing. Lets out huge SIGH of
relief.

INT. PLAYBOY MANSION GUEST HOUSE - DAY

LILY passes through kitchen area and living room, raises key
to doorknob. Heavy HUFFING and PUFFING noises stop her in her
tracks. We hear Betty HOWL. LILY knocks on door just as it
thrusts open, hits her on the forehead. FEDEX EMPLOYEE
rushes out.

                    FEDEX EMPLOYEE
          Sorry!

The room is a mess, both twin beds are unmade. BETTY's back
is to LILY as she squeezes into a pair of short shorts. PHONE
RINGS. LILY answers.

                    LILY
                 (into phone)
          Yes? Ah, well...

BETTY tosses LILY a look that reads, "You had better not!"

                    LILY (CONT'D)
               (into phone)
          ...Everything is OK. Oh I think she
          stepped on a tack or something,
          she's hopping around on one foot.

LILY offers phone receiver to BETTY.

                    LILY (CONT'D)
               (into phone)
          It's security, for you. Wants to
          know if you need first aide.

BETTY accepts and holds hand over receiver.

                    BETTY
               (whispers)
          I can't decide if you're an angel
          or a doormat.

                    LILY
               (whispers)
          You owe me.

                    LATER
          Lily and Betty sip tea in living
          room area of guest house.

                    BETTY
          So what happened, you said no to
          Hef and now you're stuck bunking
          with me?

                    LILY
          You first. Since you haven't said
          no to Hef, why are you sanctioned
          to the guest house?

Lily nibbles a shortbread cookie.

                    BETTY
          So I can order useless amounts of
          chamomile tea and cookies in order
          to check out the butler's butts,
          but most of all, handle my personal
          deliveries.

                    LILY
          You mean handle the deliverers.

                    BETTY
          Ha! I knew we'd get along just
          fine.

WHOOSH! A sudden wave of wind ploughs through living room area. Knocks a few hats off wall hat rack.

On BETTY's reaction.

                    LILY
          What's wrong?

                    BETTY
          Sometimes this place gives me the
          creeps.

BETTY rises, heads for bedroom.

                    LILY
          Hey, where you going?

With back to LILY, BETTY holds up a personal vibrator.

                    BETTY
          To take care of my nervous energy.

Alone, LILY approaches wall, fetches hats from floor, arranges them on mirrored hat rack, something catches her eye, she grabs chest, spins around.

                    LILY
          God! You scared me.

BUTLER SAM is bent over coffee table, retrieves dishes. Lily checks out his derrière.

                    LILY (CONT'D)
          I could have sworn you had long
          dark hair.

BUTLER SAM winks.

                    BUTLER SAM
          I do, on stage Wednesday nights at
          La Cage Aux Folles.

THEY CHUCKLE.

                    LILY
          So security runs a tight ship
          around here?

                    BUTLER SAM
              (winks)
          As safe as Fort Knox.

                    LILY
          Perfect!

Lily exits.

IN THE BEDROOM

LILY opens door to find BETTY partially naked, openly perched
atop her bed. She puffs on a joint with one hand, with the
other hand rubs BUZZING vibrator across-

                    LILY
          My apologies!

LILY turns on her heels with embarrassment.

                    BETTY
          No worries, the more the merrier.
          You want some of this?

                    LILY
          Oh. Well, I don't do weed-

                    BETTY
          -No, I mean...

Lily enters room, closes door behind her.

                    LILY
          You're quite the temptress, but
          look. I heard that ZouZou is the
          film for tonight's classic movie
          night, and I have nothing to wear.

INT. PLAYBOY MANSION - GREAT HALL - NIGHT

From an unknown POV on the second floor, we see LILY enter
the great hall, she pauses under the Chandelier. She wears a
beautiful vintage dress. The Chandelier flickers. JONI joins
her, holds two bowls of popcorn.

                    JONI
          Hef wants you to sit with him on
          the front couch.

INT. PLAYBOY MANSION LIVING ROOM - NIGHT

LILY enters, finds the room packed with GUESTS, some
recognizable HOLLYWOOD STARS and a few PLAYMATES. JONI guides
her to Hef's couch nearest the projection screen, where BETTY
has her hand on HEF's thigh.

                    HEF
          Wow. You look like Josephine Baker
          tonight.

LILY slides in next to BETTY. HEF puffs a joint from a
ceramic smoking stone, hands it to BETTY, who takes a drag,
offers to LILY, then takes it back, takes Lily's drag, holds
it in as she speaks.

                    BETTY
          She doesn't smoke it.

LILY grabs stone from BETTY, takes a big drag.

                    LILY
               (coughing)
          I do now.

Hef winks, rises, faces his GUESTS.

                    HEF
          It's movie time!

Everybody becomes a silhouette as the lights go out and film
projects onto the screen. As the opening credits roll, MOVIE
GUEST on LILY's right passes her bowl of popcorn, she nods a
quick thanks, when within an inch of her other ear a voice
startles her.

                    VOICE IN THE DARK
               (whispers)
          He's not for you.

LILY suspects Betty, but BETTY is engrossed with the film!

                    LILY
               (whispers)
          Did you say something?

LILY taps BETTY's arm.

                    LILY (CONT'D)
          Betty.

                    BETTY
          What!?

                    LILY
          I swear you were talking to me just
          now.

MOVIE NIGHT GUEST

SHHHH!

INT. PLAYBOY MANSION DINING ROOM - NIGHT

EVERYONE carouses over drinks and sandwiches, Hef, with Betty
draped over his arm, exits. LILY takes last chocolate chip
cookie off a lavish silver serving dish. The serving dish is
quickly replaced with another one. LILY goes for cookie
number two.

                    BUTLER SAM
          The peanut butter ones are the
          best.

                    LILY
               (munching)
          Yum, just like my grandma used to
          make.

It's obvious LILY feels a bit out of place, so SAM lingers.
From across the room, JONI catches SAM's eye. Shakes her head
no.

                    BUTLER SAM
          Sorry Lily, butlers aren't supposed
          to mix with the guests. I gotta-

But Lily's gone.

INT. PLAYBOY MANSION/PHONE ROOM - NIGHT

LILY paces, receiver at her ear, twists phone cord.

                    LILY
               (into phone)
          I just wanted to let you know I
          will be staying a little longer,
          here at the mansion.

INT. DARLA'S BEDROOM - NIGHT

On the other end of the call is DARLA, in bed.

                    DARLA
               (into phone)
          Why is that? Your apartment is
          close by, you don't need to be
          amalgamating with the likes of
          them.

INTERCUT LILY/DARLA

                    LILY
              (into phone)
         More photos-

                    DARLA
              (into phone)
         -You need to leave! I have a bad
         feeling about you being there. It's
         best you get on with your business
         and move on. Kendel's not happy
         'bout it one bit. That's for sure.

                    LILY
              (into phone)
         I told you granny Kendel and I,
         we're done. Besides, I feel safe
         here, not at my flat.

KNOCKING on phone room door.

Darla grabs her chest.

                    DARLA
              (into phone)
         Dear God Lily.

MORE KNOCKING.

                    BETTY (O.S)
         -Are you almost done in there?

                    LILY
              (into phone)
         I gotta go.

CLICK! Lily ends call. We stay on her side of the scene.

BETTY enters phone room.

                    BETTY
         Hey! I just wanted to let you know,
         I'll be upstairs with Hef, if you
         need me.

                    LILY
         Why would I need you?

                    BETTY
         I'm just saying if you're lonely,
         you can join us.

                         LILY
              I kinda ate too many cookies.
              Thanks anyway.

EXT. PLAYBOY MANSION BACK YARD - NIGHT - LATER

LILY strolls alone near the pool grotto's edge, takes a seat
on cushioned lounge. SIGHS. It starts to sprinkle. LILY lifts
up face to the receive the moisture, as if for cleansing.
Something RUSTLES in the bushes.

                         LILY
              Hello?

A movement near the bushes catches LILY's eye.

                         LILY (CONT'D)
              Anybody there?

THUD! A sudden HISS, prompts LILY to jump up, followed by a
long drawn out GROWL. LILY SCREAMS!

WE follow LILY's horrified gaze to find a decomposing feral
cat.

INT. PLAYBOY MANSION/MEDITERRANEAN ROOM - DAWN

BETTY in white terry cloth robe, LILY in a dark oversized
trench coat, whisper to each other.

                         BETTY
                    (whispers)
              What the fuck LILY.

                         LILY
                    (whispers)
              You agreed you owed me, remember?

                         BETTY
                    (whispers)
              I don't care that I helped you bury-

LILY clears her throat:

                         LILY
              Ah-uhm!

                         BETTY
                    (whispers)
              Dammit LILY, I broke a fingernail!

BUTLER MARK enters with tea-service tray.

BUTLER MARK serves tea to BETTY, then LILY. As he leans in and pours for LILY, a MUFFLED MEOW is heard.

All eyes in the room are laser-focused on the tiny black furry KITTEN nudging it's bright pink nose out from under LILY's borrowed trench coat.

                    BUTLER MARK
          Oh for God's sake.

LILY is ultra-attentive to KITTEN.

                    BUTLER MARK (CONT'D)
          Betty, your car will be here 7am.

On LILY's reaction.

                    BUTLER MARK (CONT'D)
          Double verified by security. Driver
          is on her safe list.

BUTLER MARK exits.

                    BETTY
          Gotta go fix my nail real quick.

Let's hang later, when I get back, what's your schedule today?

INT. PLAYBOY MANSION/GUEST HOUSE - DAY

IN THE LIVING ROOM

LILY admires her reflection in mirrored wall as WARDROBE ASSISTANT tacks in the waist of vintage, late 1920s, high-low hemline dress.

                    WARDROBE ASSISTANT
          Beth asked if you would consider a
          hair cut, or if not, I may have an
          avenue to acquire short wavy wigs.

                    LILY
          Hm. How about we try a wig first?

INT. PLAYBOY MANSION GUEST HOUSE - BEDROOM - NIGHT

It's pitch black. SOUNDS OF PLEASURE and SHEETS RUSTLING can be heard, then:

                    LILY
          Oh my God. Oh...Betty.

A match STRIKES, lights up room for brief moment. The twin
beds are pushed together. LILY lights a candle.

Just then the playful rescued KITTEN jumps at LILY's toes,
practices use of claws.

                    LILY (CONT'D)
               (with visible steam)
          Ouch!

LILY SNAPS on night-light, lights a cigarette on the tea
light flame then stretches her arm outward to pass cigarette.

                    LILY (CONT'D)
               (with visible steam)
          It's freezing in here. Who's going
          to keep me warm when you go out of
          town next week? Betty?

But Betty is not present.

EXT. PLAYBOY MANSION TENNIS COURT - EVENING

LILY AND BETTY in a tennis match with HEF and JAMES CAAN.

                    BETTY
               (ultra sweet)
          Sorry I couldn't get together last
          night.

                    LILY
          Your loss. I did fine without you.

There are as many looks back and forth across the net as
tennis balls. Soon they miss shots they shouldn't, except for
LILY. She kills it.

                    BETTY
               (winded)
          I need a drink.

INT. HOLMBY HILLS MANSION/GREAT HALL - NIGHT - CONTINUOUS

BETTY follows HEF up the stairs while CAAN mimes tipping his
hat off to LILY before exiting to circular driveway.

Lily makes her way to the MED ROOM deep in thought.

INT. PLAYBOY MANSION/MEDITERRANEAN ROOM - NIGHT

LILY, still in tennis clothes with small towel draped around her neck, sips from bottle of Perrier as she stares at phone. We realize LILY's attention is actually glued to small pad of HMH paper that is scribbled with the note: "He's not for you".

BUTLER SAM enters with tray of chopped salad, oil and vinegar curettes, interrupts LILY's air of doom.

                    BUTLER SAM
          Dining alone tonight.

LILY moves phone from placemat in front of her, SAM sets LILY's meal before her.

                    LILY
          Looks that way doesn't it.

The overhead light suddenly dims.

                    BUTLER SAM
          Or maybe not ha, ha.

                    LILY
          Yeah, light bulbs and I seem to
          have this thing lately.

                    BUTLER SAM
          Now that's kinky.

Lighting corrects itself.

                    LILY
          All kidding aside, how old did you
          say this place was?

Phone RINGS, startles LILY. Phone RINGS again. LILY stares at the flashing red light.

BUTLER SAM exits with:

                    BUTLER SAM
          You can answer that you know. It
          doesn't bite.

                    LILY
              (into phone with small
              voice)
          Hello?

                    SECURITY JOE
                (over phone filtered)
          Ms. Jackson. This is head of
          security, Joe Pietro. I wanted to
          make you aware that an unknown
          person on a motorcycle insisted on
          entering the gates. They were
          asking for you.

                    LILY
          The Cop.

                    SECURITY JOE
          Was not in uniform if he was. We
          refused entrance and did not
          confirm your presence.

                    LILY
          Oh.

                    SECURITY JOE
          As of yet, you have not filled out
          your safe contacts list. We take
          your privacy seriously.

                    LILY
          Thank you.

                    SECURITY JOE
          The pleasure is all mine. Good
          evening.

CLICK. LILY stares at receiver, thinks, hangs up.

                    LILY (V.O.)
          Whatever doubts I had continuing
          with this tributary in my career
          path, I was convinced, staying
          within the mansion gates was the
          safest choice. A sacrifice I must
          make.

INT. PLAYBOY MANSION/PHONE ROOM - DAY - LATER THAT WEEK

CHYRON: SHOOTING THE CENTERFOLD

One of LILY's legs with hose rolled down to high heel, toe
pointed, touching floor. The foot of her leg farthest from
camera set-up rests on small phone desk, her upper body,
leans over the task of rolling up hose, her bare breasts
exposed due to dress straps strategically placed halfway down
both arms.

Lily has a wig cap on her head. We hear a polaroid camera
SNAP, followed by a mechanical SOUND as it spits out an
instant photo. Richard compares polaroid to LILY.

                    RICHARD
          Blocking is perfect. Thank's Lily,
          you can relax for a moment.

A MAKE-UP ARTIST reaches in, applies loose powder to Lily's
face.

                    LILY
               (pouts)
          All that trouble fitting for a
          beautiful dress that doesn't even
          zip up.

HAIRDRESSER leans in places and adjusts a jet black short
wavy bobbed wig on LILY's head.

                    HAIRDRESSER
          You smell good. Chanel No.5?

LILY gets back into position, RICHARD SNAPS another polaroid.

                              INSERT POLAROID:

LILY looks exactly like her grandmother Darla did on New
Years Eve, 1928.

                              BACK TO SCENE

                    RICHARD
          Okay take five.

INT. PLAYBOY MANSION LIVING ROOM - DAY - CONTINUOUS

Alone, LILY Relaxes for a moment. A sudden room chill
encourages LILY to reach for a robe from the wardrobe rack. A
fly BUZZES, then stops. LILY feels a sting on the back of her
neck, SMACK! Checks her hand, Her breath exudes a visible
steam when she speaks.

                    LILY
               (out-loud)
          I'll get you yet, little devil.

MAKE-UP ARTIST enters.

                    MAKE-UP ARTIST
          We're ready for you. What happened
          to your neck?

INT. PLAYBOY MANSION/GUEST HOUSE BEDROOM - DAY

The room is immaculate. BUTLER SAM tidies bed pillows, LILY
latches door to rescued KITTEN's small cage.

                    BUTLER SAM
          Ready for arrival of the new
          Playmate hopefuls.

LILY hands KITTEN's cage to BUTLER SAM.

                    LILY
          I appreciate you taking care of her
          for me.

                    BUTLER SAM
          I get it, the boss prefers dogs.

INT. PLAYBOY MANSION/UPSTAIRS GUEST "RED ROOM" - DAY

LILY enters, a large bouquet of BLACK LILIES catches her
attention. She reads small card attached to floral
arrangement: "To my dear Lily, thank you for sharing your
beauty with us. All my love, Hef."

INT. PLAYBOY MANSION/MEDITERRANEAN ROOM - DAY

LILY dons the tell-tale white robe, nurses a Bloody Mary.

Two Playmate hopefuls, JAN and CYNTHIA enter.

                    CYNTHIA
          Wow, they serve alcohol for
          breakfast here?

                    LILY
          Virgin.

                    JAN
          You're a virgin? Me too.

CYNTHIA elbows JAN.

Phone RINGS, LILY answers.

                    LILY
                 (on phone)
          Yes. Sure.

LILY hangs up phone. Exits.

INT. PLAYBOY MANSION/GREAT HALL - DAY

LILY, barefoot, patters across the shiny Italian Marble floor toward stairway deep in thought.

But you didn't say no!

                    LILY
          OUCH!

LILY lifts her foot, covered in crimson blood, pulls out a piece of Art Deco crystal glass.

EXT. PLAYBOY MANSION/BACK YARD - DAY - LATER

Amidst a catered press luncheon event, LILY and CELEBRITY PSYCHIC MEDIUM contemplate LILY's palm.

                    PSYCHIC MEDIUM
          See this line here?

                    LILY
          The short one?

                    PSYCHIC MEDIUM
          Yes. That's your life line.

PSYCHIC MEDIUM frowns.

                    LILY
          What is it?

                    PSYCHIC MEDIUM
          Ah. Well. I am sorry to say you are
          in grave danger.

BETTY plops down next to LILY.

                    BETTY
          Yeah, I'm gonna kill her for
          sleeping with my boyfriend!

LILY is taken completely off guard.

                    PSYCHIC MEDIUM
          That's not something I would brag
          about. Who is this Boyfriend?

                    BETTY
              (smug)
          Mr. Hugh Hefner himself.

                    PSYCHIC MEDIUM
              You mean Hef?

BETTY follows PSYCHIC MEDIUM's gaze where cameras flash at
HEF who is dressed in a denim suit, sandwiched between JAN
and CYNTHIA.

LILY extends both palms in front of her, flips them over,
notices some dried blood around finger nails on her right
hand. Troubled, she jolts out of her seat.

                    LILY
              Excuse me ladies.

LILY scampers off.

                    BETTY
                 (to Psychic Medium)
              Gee wiz, she didn't have to get her
              panties in a knot, I was only
              kidding.

                    PSYCHIC MEDIUM
              Before you jumped in we were
              discussing her Black Moon Lilith,
              where it's located in her birth
              chart.

                    BETTY
              Meaning what?

                    PSYCHIC MEDIUM
              I've seen you two interact before,
              you seem quite close. You best be
              careful, you are most likely
              already experiencing it. Would you
              like me to give you a reading?

BETTY, distracted by what Hef is up to across the lawn,
offers her palm to PSYCHIC MEDIUM.

INT. PLAYBOY MANSION/GREAT HALL - DAY

LILY scans the marble floor as she limps toward staircase.

INT. PLAYBOY MANSION/UPSTAIRS GUEST "RED ROOM" - EVENING

In the EN SUITE bathroom, LILY scrubs finger nails with nail
brush. Suddenly, "Brown Sugar" by the Rolling Stones BLARES
from bedroom clock radio. By the look on LILY's face, we know
she hates the song.

MICK JAGERS'S VOICE

-Just around midnight! Brown sugar! How come you taste so
good? Brown Sugar! Just like a young girl should.

BAM! LILY strikes clock radio, then pulls out plug. She lets
out a hearty exhale of VISIBLE STEAM.

A FED-EX envelope is slipped under the door. LILY rushes to
door, retrieves envelope, reads label smiles. We see the
label with the return address of JACK PARK.

LILY tares open envelope. Her exuberance turns to shock as
she focuses on a photo, she drops it on the bed. Reads
included note.

                    JACK (V.O.)
          I thought you would enjoy this
          photo I snapped of your grandma and
          the hostess of the New Year's Eve
          party we attended in 1928. Hope all
          is well. Love, Jack.

LILY grabs phone, pushes zero.

                    LILY
               (into phone)
          Can I get an outside line? Yes,
          Lily.

PLAYBOY MANSION/ GUEST "RED ROOM" - DAY

                    LILY
               (into phone)
          Alabama. Okay thank you.

DARLA's KITCHEN - DAY

Darla is chopping herbs into fine pieces atop the center
island wood block. Phone RINGS. DARLA grabs receiver, tucks
it under her ear, swivels back to wood block, continues
activity while conversing.

                    DARLA
               (into phone)
          As I live and breath! Thought maybe
          the cat got your tongue.

                         INTERCUT
                         LILY/DARLA:

                    LILY
              (into phone)
          Sorry, been real busy.

                    DARLA
              (into phone)
          Acting?

                    LILY
              (into phone)
          I'm cursed.

                    DARLA
              (into phone)
          Now why the devil would you ask
          that?

                    LILY
              (into phone)
          Because of my name. Because of my
          heritage?

                    DARLA
              (into phone)
          Lily is a sweet name, child.

LILY continues to exude a new personality trait. Terse.

                    LILY
              (into phone)
          Come on, cut the bull, it's Lilith.
          Why did you insist I would be named
          Lilith?

                    DARLA
              (into phone)
          Now hold up a minute missy!

                    LILY
              (sneering into phone)
          Tell me. Or is it another one of
          your dark secrets. How exactly do
          you and Jack go way back?
              (beat)
          I'm sitting here looking at photos.

No answer.

                    LILY (CONT'D)
              (into phone)
          Forget it. Just explain to me what
          Black Moon Lilith represents.

Now Darla is pissed. CHOPS herbs a bit faster.

                    DARLA
               (into phone)
          Seems you got it down pat already,
          since you clearly are expressing
          the dark side of your personality.
          I think it's best we end this call.

                    LILY
               (into phone)
          No! Something is happening to me
          and I need your help. I need to
          know who the hell Amanda is to you.

DARLA reacts, cuts her finger.

                    DARLA
               (into phone)
          Since you insist. When in your
          "chart", Black Moon Lilith
          represents a person's primitive
          impulses and behavior in their
          rawest form.

                    LILY
               (into phone)
          Go on.
               (beat)
          Say it!

                    DARLA
               (into phone)
          Listen miss attitude, why are you
          asking me? You already know the
          answers.

DARLA applies first aide to finger.

                    LILY
               (into phone)
          I want to hear you say it.

                    DARLA
               (into phone)
          Where it is in your chart can
          actually determine possible hidden
          sexual fantasies and secret
          fetishes, and, may I remind you, is
          the reason why you have to leave
          that place, bad shit is gonna
          happen!

                    LILY
                (into phone)
          Bad shit is already happening,
          that's why I'm still here.

Sound of phone CLICK then a dial TONE in DARLA's ear.

                    DARLA
                (into phone)

LILY? LILY?

The call ends and we stay on Darla's side of the scene. DARLA
dials phone base with earnest. With phone receiver to ear,
she hears a telephone company recorded messaged.

                    RECORDED MESSAGE
                (over the phone filtered)
          The phone number you have dialed is
          out of service at this time. Please
          try-

                                        JUMP CUT TO:

INT. PLAYBOY MANSION/UPSTAIRS GUEST "RED ROOM" - EVENING

IN THE ENSUITE BATH ROOM

LILY shaves her legs. It's clear she is in an odd mood. Hums
to tune of "Brown Sugar".

IN THE BEDROOM

LILY unties her silk robe in front of a full length mirror,
lets it drop to the floor. She admires and adjusts her
somewhat see-through sexy lingerie.

She rolls up stockings, clips to garter belt. Her exhale
breaths display VISIBLE STEAM. Her nipples harden, visible
underneath the bra's mesh fabric. LILY pulls tight dress over
her head, straps on high heels, exits.

INT. PLAYBOY MANSION/MASTER BEDROOM - NIGHT

HEF and BETTY relax on bed in white robes, facing large video
screen. Light from the moving images on screen flickers on
their faces. They nibble on late, late, dinners from
individual bed trays nestled over their bodies. LILY, still
fully clothed, is painting Betty's toenails red.

                    HEF
          Have you decided yet Lily?

LILY does't answer.

                    HEF (CONT'D)
          You know how important you are to
          me, don't you?

                    BETTY
          Us.

                    LILY
          Yes.

                    HEF
          Then it is settled.

Hef points to his cheek, his eyes locked on video screen,
mesmerized by a scene from Dracula (1931).

                    LILY
          I'll pick up the rest of my stuff.

LILY kisses Hef's cheek, exits.

EXT. WESTWOOD APARTMENT BUILDING - DAY

It's raining.

A BLACK LIMO pulls up to the curb. LIMO DRIVER exits vehicle,
opens umbrella then passenger door, offers his hand to LILY.

On the second floor we see LILY dressed like a movie star.
Her hair tucked under head scarf. Despite the weather she
wears sunglasses.

LILY reaches for door knob to insert key.

Door is ajar!

LILY slowly pushes door in.

                    LILY
                 (nervous)
          Hello?

It's pitch dark inside.

                    LILY (CONT'D)
          Jack? Is that you Jack?

No answer. LILY's heels CLICK on the floor as she crosses
room. She FLICKS on wall sconce light. LILY CLICKS over to
dresser mirror, takes off scarf and sunglasses, leans into
mirror to check her puffy under-eyes, and BOOM! KENDEL pops
up behind her.

                    LILY (CONT'D)
          FUCK! Kendel, what are you doing
          here?

                    KENDEL
               (sneers)
          Just that. I'm here to fuck, then
          take you home.

Lily pushes Kendel aside, gathers and bags a few items.

                    KENDEL (CONT'D)
          Who the hell is Jack by the way?

Lily ignores him, focussing on her exodus.

                    KENDEL (CONT'D)
          Since when did you start cussing?
               (beat)
          You are such a whore.

LILY goes to slap KENDEL, he grabs her wrist mid-air. LILY's
eyes flare with mixed emotions.

                    LILY
               (snarls)
          He's my eighty-five year old
          landlord you stupid son-of-a-bitch!

KENDEL whirls LILY around, pushes her up against the wall,
RIP! Off comes her dress and WAM! WAM! WAM! LILY relives her
re-occurring nightmare in the flesh. The wall sconce light
FLICKERS. LILY has a surge of energy, overcomes KENDEL,
pushes him to ground, straddles atop his lower waist.

                    DARKNESS
          In total control, LILY grunts
          enthusiastically. Everything is out
          of focus except for LILY's face of
          complete satisfaction and power as
          she brings KENDEL with her to full-
          blown orgasm!

                    KENDEL
          Oh...my...God!

                                        SMASH CUT TO:

EXT. WESTWOOD APARTMENT BUILDING - DAY

Sunlight peaks through the overhead clouds.

LILY whips around the corner with a bag of stuff in each hand
with Kendel at her heels continuing their argument.

                    LILY
          Never! I wish you were dead!

                    KENDEL
          Lily. Lily! Wait, I only showed up
          unannounced, because I'm worried
          about you! Darla is worried about
          you!

DRIVER opens limo door for LILY.

                    KENDEL (CONT'D)
               (to driver)
          Who the fuck are you?!

LILY enters limo, DRIVER closes door, avoiding contact with
KENDEL. The DRIVER makes their way to driver side of vehicle.

KENDEL POUNDS on LILY's window, as limo take off.

Suddenly a mangy looking MAN bumps into KENDEL. KENDEL WHIPS
around to see MAN clutching Kendel's wallet.

                    KENDEL (CONT'D)
          Hey!

MAN darts across street.

INT./EXT. LIMO - TRAVELING - DAY

Limo, pulls away from curb, DRIVER adjusts rear-view-mirror.

                    DRIVER
          Jealous boyfriend?

From DRIVER's POV we see LILY shrug, as she applies lipstick,
a BUS is also seen through limo's rear window.

                              SMASH CUT TO:

EXT. STREET IN FRONT OF WESTWOOD APARTMENT BUILDING - DAY

In his attempt to catch the pick-pocket, KENDEL darts into
street, oblivious of the bus, and SMACK!

INT. LOS ANGELES COUNTY MORGUE - DAY

Coroner checks tag that reads "John Doe. DOA", that is
attached to a bruised black man's foot that sticks out from
under lumpy blanket.

Coroner slides Kendel's body tray into wall storage.

                              FADE OUT.

EXT. PLAYBOY MANSION/BACKYARD - DAY - MONTHS LATER

With full blown spring colors, the landscape bursts with new
life. On the left, peacocks lift their chests, and spread
their tail feathers, as do some of the NEWER PLAYMATES.

The center lawn boasts a tent under which a petting zoo of
baby farm animals and, yes, reptiles, are literally up for
grabs.

Behind the tent, in front of the small stream at the base of
embankment that angles upward to fenced property line, a
topless woman's pasties twirl about as she springs up and
down from a trampoline.

The woman stops when offered a pastel colored robe.

                    BUTLER MARK
          Keep it PG. Families will be
          arriving in ten.

INT. PLAYBOY MANSION KITCHEN - DAY

Bustling with food prep activities, the KITCHEN STAFF finish
final touches, BUTLERS enter and exit with trays of food.

LILY, dressed in her Sunday best, pushes through the Med Room
entrance to kitchen, makes sharp left where she opens and
closes a few cupboards. BUTLER DAN, on his way to the Med
Room exit, with tray of chip and dip, pauses.

                    BUTLER DAN
          Need some Help?

LILY smiles, grabs a chip.

                    LILY
               (crunching)
          I wanted a real glass for my
          mimosa.

LILY holds up crystal art decor champaign glass.

                    BUTLER DAN
          That cupboard is off limits, but I
          suppose it won't matter since you
          seem to be the lady of the house.

LILY blushes. Shakes head.

                    LILY
          Not quite sure who Hef's main
          squeeze is these days, there's been
          so many.

                    BUTLER DAN
          In that case use plastic, it is
          safest with these large events.

BUTLER DAN exits. LILY sticks out her tongue.

EXT. PLAYBOY MANSION VERANDA BAR - DAY

LILY continues to munch on chips as BUTLER SAM, tops off her
mimosa.

                    LILY
          There was only one of these in the
          cupboard, I'm sure it won't be
          missed.

BUTLER SAM winks at LILY, as he adds a sprig of mint.

                    BUTLER SAM
          For the breath.

                    BETTY
          Hey stranger!

BETTY's arms reach out for LILY, they hug, LILY pulls back.

                    LILY
          Oh dear.

They GIGGLE as LILY gently touches BETTY's pregnancy bump.

                    LILY (CONT'D)
          You look beautiful.

FEDEX EMPLOYEE, dressed in white suit, slips his hand into
BETTY's, smiles. A proud dad-to-be.

LILY sips mimosa, BETTY stiffens when she notices the crystal
champagne glass.

                    BETTY
          Well it was nice to see you.

BETTY and her baby daddy exit in haste.

LILY shrugs.

                    LILY
               (to Butler Sam)
          Must be her hormones.

LILY descends a few steps to yard level, where a row of
carnival like kiosks catches her attention. Hot dog stand,
ice cream station, and a vintage popcorn wagon. She choses
line beside hot dog stand.

LILY takes notice of HEF talking with someone in the yard.
From behind, the woman has long black flowing hair.

                    LILY (CONT'D)
               (to herself)
          Who is that woman?

A sudden and unexpected answer startles LILY.

                    BETTY
          My mid-wife!

                    LILY
          Jesus, where did you come from?

BETTY places finger to her lips.

                    BETTY
          Shh!

BETTY slips her hand into LILY's.

                    BETTY (CONT'D)
          I want to show you something. To
          take your mind off everything.

INT. PLAYBOY MANSION/INDOOR BIRD SANCTUARY - DAY

LILY and BETTY pull out of a heated kiss. As LILY gives
BETTY's engorged breasts one last kiss before tucking them
away. BETTY's mood takes quick one-eighty.

                    BETTY
          I want to remind you Hef is mine.
          You will never be his main
          girlfriend.
                    (MORE)

                    BETTY (CONT'D)
          Just because you fuck around here
          and there with other women, doesn't
          make you special. Your refusal to
          engage in threesomes...

On LILY's dumbfounded reaction.

                    BETTY (CONT'D)
               (sneers)
          ...That's right sister. Why do you
          think all my stuff is still in the
          master bedroom. You don't even have
          a date set for your centerfold do
          you?

A colorful parrot SQUAWKS.

                    PARROT
          Squawk! He's not for you! Squawk!
          He's not for you!

                    BETTY
               (face distorts with
               anger)
          Ditto! I am the one who brings the
          new girls to his bed. I organize
          the orgies. I am the one who makes
          sure-

                    LILY
          -I am not interested in being
          anyones girlfriend! It was one and
          done, that was the agreement. I
          don't understand, you're hear with-

                    BETTY
          -Let me spell it out for you then.

Several exotics birds are outside their cages.

                    BETTY (CONT'D)
          Me and baby daddy are here to fuck
          Hef! And you're not invited! In
          fact. I'm gonna make sure you are
          kicked off the property for good!

LILY tears up.

                    LILY
          No. Betty, you promised.

BETTY flips LILY off with middle finger.

                    BETTY
          That's what I think about your not
          so little secret!

All birds SCREECHING. LILY COVERS her ears, runs out.

EXT. PLAYBOY MANSION POOLSIDE GROTTO BAR - DAY

Crowded with MANSION GUESTS.

LILY sucks down a shot of whiskey from clear plastic cup.

                    LILY
               (to bar-tender)
          Another!

Distant SCREAMING. From LILY's POV we follow the horror
displayed on MANSION GUEST's faces to the source of SCREAMS.

It's BETTY, covered in blood streaming from several wounds
inflicted by EXOTIC BIRDS pecking her face and arms! BETTY
misses short flight of steps, falls face first, SPLAT!

EXT. PLAYBOY MANSION BACK YARD - DAY - HOURS LATER

The yard has been cleared of the day's festivities, horrors,
and guests.

A DETECTIVE SIMMS, speaks with LILY.

                    DETECTIVE SIMMS
          We know you were close, but she was
          a troubled young woman. Security
          has provided video footage of her
          and that fella, pouring something
          in the bird feeders, and unlocking
          the cages. You were clearly the
          intended victim.

LILY looks up as Mr. FEDEX EMPLOYEE, in cuffs, is escorted by
a POLICE OFFICER.

                    LILY
          There are cameras?

SQUAWK! LILY turns her attention toward the sound. The sun in
her eyes, she squints to discern the shape of a WOMAN WITH
FLOWING BLACK HAIR, the same woman she saw when taking the
horse photographs, the same woman, Amanda, with her grandma,
Darla, in the photograph.

One of the loose exotic birds rests on the WOMAN WITH FLOWING
BLACK HAIR'S shoulder, it SQUAWKS, takes off in flight.

                    LILY (CONT'D)
          Who is that woman? She looks allot
          like - have you questioned her?

DETECTIVE SIMMS follows LILY's line of sight.

                    DETECTIVE SIMMS
          What woman? I suggest you take it
          easy. It's been a rough afternoon.

DETECTIVE SIMMS hands lily a business card.

                    DETECTIVE SIMMS (CONT'D)
               (frowns)
          Just in case you need me.

INT. PLAYBOY MANSION GREAT HALL - EVENING

LILY, despondent, enters, as last of the afternoon guests
exit to the circular driveway. She spots a young, beautiful
Asian woman, VICTORIA WONG, 20s, receive a kiss on the lips
from HEF. LILY rushes up stairs past them.

INT. PLAYBOY MANSION/UPSTAIRS GUEST "RED ROOM" - NIGHT

LILY frantically packs clothes from dresser drawers into
carpet bag. Stops, thinks. With reluctance places clothes
back in drawers. KNOCK! KNOCK! KNOCK! LILY jumps out of her
skin, her face looses color. A softer KNOCK, KNOCK, on the
door is followed by a sing-song, saccharin-sweet voice.

                    VICTORIA
               (softly)
          Lily? Lily, can I come in?

LILY checks her reflection in mirror, doesn't care that the
SHADOW OF AMANDA's GHOST darts behind her.

                    LILY
          Just a minute.

LILY closes dresser drawer, crosses over, opens door.
VICTORIA slides in. LILY is mesmerized by her beauty.

                    VICTORIA
          I came to cheer you up.

VICTORIA hands lily a cupcake, giggles. LILY studies the
pastel frosting covered in tiny circular sprinkles. VICTORIA
points to the purple one in the center.

                    VICTORIA (CONT'D)
          That's purple micro-dot.

                    LILY
          A new flavor?

                    VICTORIA
          No, I'm already Miss June. Have you
          ever taken acid? Hef and I would
          like you to join us. In the
          bedroom.

Phone RINGS. LILY hesitates, then picks up receiver.

                    LILY
               (into phone)
          Hello?

                    DETECTIVE SIMMS
               (over phone filtered)
          Ms. Jackson?

No answer.

                    DETECTIVE SIMMS (CONT'D)
               (over phone filtered)
          Ms. Jackson? This is Detective
          Simms, we spoke earlier today.

                    LILY
               (into phone)
          Oh, yes. Hello.

                    DETECTIVE SIMMS
               (over phone filtered)
          I was wondering, if you could come
          down to the station.

Nervous, LILY licks frosting off the cupcake without
thinking. Wall lights FLICKER.

                    LILY
               (into phone)
          Station? I thought I answered all
          your questions this afternoon. You
          said the case was closed.

                    DETECTIVE SIMMS
               (over phone filtered)
          Yes, but something else has come to
          my attention.

                              J-CUT TO:

BEVERLY HILLS POLICE STATION - NIGHT

On the other end of the call DETECTIVE SIMMS shuffles papers
as COP CORY studies detective's every word.

                    DETECTIVE SIMMS
               (into phone)
          Something that I would prefer to
          see you in person about.

COP CORY nods his head in approval.

                    LILY
               (over phone filtered)
          Can't you come back here to see me?

                    DETECTIVE SIMMS
               (into phone)
          No, well see, that's just it. This
          is something that is developing
          outside the Playboy Mansion
          Grounds, so I am not authorized to
          enter the grounds at this time. It
          would be purely voluntary on your
          part. To come in to the station
          that is.

MOTORCYCLE COP throws hands in the air, pissed.

                    LILY
               (over phone, filtered)
          Oh. Okay. In that case, if it's not
          an urgent matter. I'd prefer not.

CLICK! DETECTIVE SIMMS shrugs.

                    DETECTIVE SIMMS
               (to Cop Cory)
          I'm going to need more evidence.

INT. PLAYBOY MANSION MASTER BATHROOM - NIGHT

LILY and VICTORIA make a mess with too much bubble bath. LILY
flings a wad of soap bubbles at VICTORIA.

From LILY's LSD induced POV we see soap bubbles soar,
twinkle, and land on VICTORIA's head like falling stars.

                              CUT TO:

PLAYBOY MANSION MASTER BEDROOM - NIGHT

A long drawn-out series of SWIRLING BODY PARTS and RAPTUROUS
MOANS as LILY is indoctrinated into the world of three-somes.

Or was there four?

INT. PLAYBOY MANSION GREAT HALL - DAY - WEEKS LATER

LILY hugs VICTORIA, who wears the black and white PLAYMATE
PROMOTION gear of the ERA. Look of concern on VICTORIA's
face. A moment of secret discussion transpires.

                    VICTORIA
          You need to figure something out.
          Hef mentioned Beth and he are
          discussing my Playmate of the Year
          pictorial.

                    LILY
          Congratulations, that's what you
          want isn't it?

                    VICTORIA
               (serious)
          They want me to reshoot everything
          you have already done.

They dis-embrace as Hef enters Great Hall.

Hef lowers chin, lights pipe. With eyes like black raisins he
peers though PUFFS of pipe smoke, clearly sizing up LILY to
VICTORIA.

He joins VICTORIA, kisses her on top of the head.

                    VICTORIA (CONT'D)
               (giggles)
          See you tonight! Lily said she'd
          join us, right Lily?

                    HEF
          That won't be necessary. She's been
          under the weather.

LILY is shocked they speak of her in the third person. HEF
notices LILY's discomfort.

                    HEF (CONT'D)
          Isn't that right LILY?

VICTORIA makes face gestures behind Hef's back to prompt LILY
to save her status.

                    LILY
               (sheepish smile)
          -Uhm. I'm better now?

                    HEF
          You're not too occupied with
          research?

                    LILY
          Sir?

                    HEF
          Mansion fables?

                    VICTORIA
               (to Hef)
          Please?

HEF takes a hearty PUFF off pipe, exits with:

                    HEF
          Sure.
               (chuckles)
          Why not invite your ghost as well?

EXT. PLAYBOY MANSION CIRCULAR DRIVEWAY - DAY

LILY steps out front Door, VICTORIA slides in back of LIMO,
waves. As the LIMO pulls away, LILY does a double take. The
GHOST OF AMANDA's face appears in the back window of the limo
next to VICTORIA's.

EXT. PLAYBOY MANSION POOL/INT. KOREA TOWN RESTAURANT - DAY

INTERCUT

AT THE PLAYBOY MANSION POOL

LILY, JAN and CYNTHIA float on pool's surface with rafts.
Only JAN wears a bathing suit.

                    CYNTHIA
          Tan-lines are a pin-up's worst
          enemy.

                    JAN
          I think they can be sexy, with the
          correct lighting.

                    CYNTHIA
          What's your excuse LILY? I've never
          seen you so bold.

AT THE KOREAN RESTAURANT

VICTORIA signs autograph on Playmate promo head-shot for a
FAN, as WAITER waits patiently to serve her food. FAN leaves,
Victoria tucks napkin in her blouse, WAITER places bowl of
kimichi before her.

                    VICTORIA
          That smells so good! I am starving.

AT THE PLAYBOY MANSION POOL

From LILY's POV we see HEF in his second story window, gaze
back at her approvingly.

                    LILY
          Seems my prudish ways were
          diminishing my chances for
          publication.

LILY pushes her raft closer to back edge of pool so HEF can
have a better view of her. He does, he smiles.

AT THE KOREAN RESTAURANT

Victoria digs in. A couple of FANS come out of the woodwork
to snap some photos of her mowing down her lunch. Irritated
VICTORIA covers her face with her arm, YELLS.

                    VICTORIA
          No paparazzi!

She HICCUPS. A FAN ignores her wishes, leans in with camera.

                    VICTORIA (CONT'D)
          I said no photos while I-

VICTORIA projectile vomits all over the FAN.

                    VICTORIA (CONT'D)
                (choking)
          Oh, God, I'm so sorry-

AT THE PLAYBOY MANSION POOL

Sudden RUSTLE in bushes, causes LILY to fall off raft. She comes up for air, witnesses HEF's SHEEPDOG digging earth.

                    LILY
          No! BAD DOG!

AT THE KOREAN RESTAURANT

RESTAURANT PATRONS SCREAM as VICTORIA bolts up out of chair, FLATULENCE EXPLODES from her body. A GRUESOME sight, PATRONS knock over tables in order to escape the horror, VICTORIA's body SPASMS amongst her excrement on the floor, until lifeless.

AT THE PLAYBOY MANSION POOL

SHEEPDOG digs with crazed enthusiasm. Then YELPS in PAIN.

As LILY pushes her dripping wet body from pool to grab a towel, she catches glimpse of AMANDA'S GHOST. SHEEPDOG BARKS.

                    END INTERCUT

INT. PLAYBOY MANSION MASTER BEDROOM - NIGHT

HEF and LILY lay atop the bed in white robes. HEF, clearly not interested in LILY, reads newspaper with a frown. LILY takes a puff off joint before she snubs it out in bedside ashtray.

                    LILY
          I'm sure Victoria will have a
          reasonable explanation.

No answer.

                    LILY (CONT'D)
          I was wondering if it would be ok
          if I had a seance on the property?

Still no answer.

                    LILY (CONT'D)
          Ok, well. I've got the munchies.

LILY slides off bed, removes white robe which exposes her fully clothed body, exits.

INT. PLAYBOY MANSION/KITCHEN - NIGHT

Soft light emotes from the large commercial freezer. LILY
moves some items around for a mid-night raid of Haagen-Dazs
ice-cream. A dark shadow moves behind her. Satisfied of her
choice, LILY closes large freezer door, and BOOM! Sam, tray
in hand, is dumbfounded by her reaction as shadow flits off
behind him.

                    LILY
          Shit Sam! You scared the hell of
          me. What are you doing here?

                    BUTLER SAM
          Hef wants to retire early, he
          moved his 2am dinner up to 12:30
          am.

BUTLER SAM focuses on pint of ice-cream in LILY's possession.

                    BUTLER SAM (CONT'D)
          Give me a buzz here in the kitchen,
          later, if you need something more
          substantial to eat.

INT. PLAYBOY MANSION/UPSTAIRS GUEST "RED ROOM" - NIGHT

Alone, LILY finishes off ice-cream, retrieves a fresh joint
from robe pocket, lights and smokes, passes out.

BEGIN LILY'S DREAM

INT. CHURCH OF THE LATTER-DAY SAINTS/COAT CLOSET - DAY

                    CHYRON: 1928
          Between the overcoats, up against a
          wall of LDS POSTERS, we see DARLA,
          her upper body fully clothed, she
          leans back in ECSTASY. She smiles
          as her lover AMANDA comes up for
          air and a kiss.

They rotate during passionate kiss, Darla dives down out of
sight. AMANDA stiffens and SQUEALS.

END LILY's DREAM

The room's red velvet walls glow from the sconce lights near
the ceiling that encases the kingsize bed with Lily, asleep
on her stomach in nothing but her birthday suit.

The satin sheet slowly moves upward to cover LILY, without
LILY's help!

She BREATHES HEAVILY, arches the satin sheet upward and
downward with the rise and fall of her buttocks engulfing her
hand until:

                         LILY
               Ahhhhhhhhhh.

The iPod pops on with the Roy Fox tune "It's Got to Be Love."

LILY rolls over on her back. The radios SNAPS OFF. Her eyes
pop open.

                                        JUMP CUT TO:

INT. PLAYBOY MANSION/"RED ROOM"/ENSUITE BATHROOM - NIGHT

A large pair of sharp scissors comes into frame -- points
straight at LILY's head! LILY grabs the scissors.

                         BUTLER SAM
               Are you sure you want to do this?

We see LILY's catatonic reflection in the mirror as she SNIPS
her hair off. A shadow overcomes bathroom lighting.

                         LILY
               I noticed Hef's weakness for
               nostalgia. If he liked my wig,
               he'll adore my hairstyle.

                         BUTLER SAM
               You're sure?

                         LILY
               Whatever I can do to get him to
               change his mind.

BUTLER SAM gives LILY a look.

                         LILY (CONT'D)
               Besides sex. Also, I want to
               arrange a seance on the property.

                         BUTLER SAM
               I am surprised you haven't noticed
               already, any extra curricular
               activity on these grounds is theme-
               based. That said, a seance is only
               allowed at the annual Halloween
               Party.

                    LILY
          I cant wait that long. I need to
          know want she wants. She
          infiltrates my dreams, and
          embarrassing as it is for me to
          admit, my fantasies. This has been
          going on ever since I came to
          Hollywood.

LILY searches BUTLER SAM's face for answers.

                    BUTLER SAM
          You said you are a good actress.
          Play the part. With him, I mean.
          The ghost of Mrs. Letts, that's a
          different story, with that my
          friend, you are playing with fire.

Sam exits, LILY shapes her hair with product, approves her
reflection in the mirror. Vanity Lightbulb flashes.

INT. PLAYBOY MANSION/MEDITERRANEAN ROOM - MORNING

LILY, in her new -- exactly like Darla's circa 1928 haircut --
sips a cup of tea, picks up Newspaper with a look of shock.

LILY reads out-loud...

                              INSERT NEWSPAPER
                              HEADLINE:

"PLAYBOY MODEL VICTORIA WONG DIES HORRIBLE DEATH"

EXT. PLAYBOY MANSION - DAY

LILY, crumpled up in a physical knot atop second floor
balcony, wears a stone-cold lifeless look of exhaustion on
her face and a thin silk slip on her body.

Through LILY's catatonic pov, we see JAN doing cartwheels
around CYNTHIA who sunbathes topless on the great lawn.

From JAN's POV, the horrifically magical world of the Playboy
Mansion is right side up and wrong side down, as it twirls
gloriously around and around and around-

                    CYNTHIA
          Stop it!

JAN plops on the grass at Cynthia's command. JAN's VISUAL
signs of DIZZINESS, pisses CYNTHIA off even more. WHAP!

JAN immediately straightens out, thanks to CYNTHIA's bright
red open palm.

                    CYNTHIA (CONT'D)
          Now look what you made me do. The
          childish ways you accomplish
          feeling out of it can be realized
          with a single pill.

CYNTHIA retrieves a thick white pill from locket around her
neck. Pops it in her mouth.

                    CYNTHIA (CONT'D)
          Quaalude! Hand me a PEPSI will ya?

But JAN is busy icing her face, fixated on LILY in the
distance.

                    JAN
          I'm worried about her. Even though
          Victoria died of food poisoning,
          she's convinced it was her fault.
          She seems so lonely.

Irritated, CYNTHIA bounces up off blanket, grabs PEPSI from
cooler, lops off cap with opener, turns her attention to LILY
as she CHUGS down liquid, some drizzles down her bare,
reddened, chest.

                    CYNTHIA
          She's not alone. She been hanging
          with that long, dark-haired lady
          since we met her.

                    JAN
          You mean Hef's secretary Joni?

                    CYNTHIA
          No stupid, that lady, see?

Cynthia points her PEPSI bottle toward the second floor
balcony window, behind LILY, where we see AMANDA, now a
shadow then--

                    JAN
          Where? I don't see anyone?!

Cynthia shrugs.

                    CYNTHIA
          All I know is LILY loves pussy, and
          she hasn't left that room for days.
          If she's not doing that dark haired
          lady, she must be jonesing!

                    JAN
          Do you think she's screwing the
          ghost of Mrs. Letts?

                    CYNTHIA
          What the hell are you talking
          about?

                    JAN
          Well LILY told me I would still be
          a virgin even if I masturbated
          while fantasizing about someone.

                    CYNTHIA
          Really.

                    JAN
          Yep. She told me she does it all
          the time. She told me she sees a
          woman with flowing dark hair in a
          white dress.

JUNE and CYNTHIA gather their stuff. CYNTHIA pulls on a t-
shirt, gazes up toward empty second floor balcony.

                    CYNTHIA
          Hmm. Sounds Kinky. Lily's right, we
          gotta have a seance.

LILY pops out of nowhere, Cynthia jumps out of her skin.

                    CYNTHIA (CONT'D)
          You scared the shit out of me!

LILY shoots eye daggers at CYNTHIA.

                    CYNTHIA (CONT'D)
          I'm so sorry, bad choice of words.

                    LILY
          I already asked security, they said
          we'd have to wait till after 4th of
          July celebration tomorrow and get
          Hef's approval for the seance.

                    JAN
          And?

                    LILY
          I'm working on it. Got any more
          qualudes?

                    CYNTHIA
          In our room. We are here for ya
          babe.

EXT. PLAYBOY MANSION/BACKYARD - NIGHT

Full blown fourth of July Celebration!

HEF's new favorite Playmate, MARSHA, 20's, snuggles next to
him, then BOOM! BOOM! BOOM! The FINALE FIREWORKS glisten in
the night sky. POUF! What looks like a FIREBALL blows up on
the backyard's security fence! Disneyland grade fireworks
plummet the night sky. LILY, JAN, CYNTHIA, HEF's GUESTS,
PLAYMATES and their FAMILIES enjoy the show from white
folding chairs. OOHS and AAHS weave in between CELEBRATORY
MUSIC. A grand fourth of July.

INT. PLAYBOY MANSION/GREAT HALL - DAY - LATER

CYNTHIA enters great hall to find LILY, visibly shaken,
chatting with security.

                    SECURITY JOE
          Will have to wait till morning to
          exhume the rest of the body. A
          Detective Simms informed me she'll
          be here as well, says she needs to
          corroborate some witness
          statements, ask some questions.

CYNTHIA thinks twice, tucks something in her bra, continues
through veranda toward back yard.

                    SECURITY JOE (CONT'D)
          Excuse me.

Security Joe joins FIRE MARSHAL at the veranda bar.

                    LILY
               (to her-self)
          Shit, shit, shit, shit!

JAN joins LILY.

                    JAN
          Hey, did we get the approval?

JAN follows LILY's fixed gaze at Hef's SHEEPDOG, who stares
right back at them with a panting doggy smile, proud of his
findings as it rolls toward LILY and JAN...

                    JAN (CONT'D)
          EW!

A human eyeball!

INT. PLAYBOY MANSION/MEDITERRANEAN ROOM - DAY

MARSHA holds court with all current PLAYMATE HOPEFULS over
coffee. LILY is pleasant as possible, more curious with what
she can see transpiring in GREAT HALL through open connecting
door.

CSI in HAZMAT suits wheel out BODY.

JAN and a few others speak to LILY, but their words fall upon
deaf ears. Instead, LILY rises from chair, mesmerized by
vision of WOMAN WITH LONG FLOWING BLACK HAIR, AMANDA,
hovering over staircase. LILY exits, moves through GREAT
HALL, trance-like to foot of stairs, where she is interrupted
by:

                    DETECTIVE SIMMS
          Ms. Jackson!

LILY comes back to realty, smiles sweetly.

                    LILY
          Oh, hi detective.

                    DETECTIVE SIMMS
          Good to see you healthy and
          smiling. I must admit I was
          concerned last week, when I
          couldn't get through to you here. I
          guess you took me off your safe
          list. Can we go somewhere more
          private to talk?

INT. PLAYBOY MANSION/LIVING ROOM - DAY

LILY and DETECTIVE SIMMS plop on large leather couch. LILY
grabs wooden bowl thats rests on table behind them, she
offers detective some M&M's.

                    DETECTIVE SIMMS
          Thanks. The blue ones are my
          favorite.

DETECTIVE SIMMS picks out a few BLUE M&M's.

                    DETECTIVE SIMMS (CONT'D)
               (crunching)
          A cop from my precinct tipped me
          off to your apartment building, so
          I spoke with a Jack Park.

                    LILY
               (innocent)
          -Am I under arrest?

                    DETECTIVE SIMMS
               (laughs)
          Oh Lord no. Why would you think
          that?

                    LILY
               (sweet)
          Because I didn't come forward when
          you called me to come in?

                    DETECTIVE SIMMS
               (illusive)
          No dear, I just wanted to warn you.
          Mr. Park said you have a very
          pissed of Grandmother coming to
          town.

DETECTIVE SIMMS rises.

                    LILY
          Thanks for the heads up. I
          appreciate it.

LILY rises, offers hand to shake with DETECTIVE SIMMS, who
doesn't accept.

                    DETECTIVE SIMMS
          The other something else we will
          wrap up soon.

                    LILY
          Oh.

                    DETECTIVE SIMMS
          Yesterday, an over-jealous
          motorcycle cop, the one insisting I
          bring you in for questioning, same
          fella who gave me the tip, wound up
          frying himself trying to climb over
          the back yard security fence here
          last night.

DETECTIVE SIMMS is not able to read LILY's reaction.

                    DETECTIVE SIMMS (CONT'D)
          You still have my business card? I
          may need you to come in and answer
          some questions. I'll let you know.

DETECTIVE SIMMS winks, exits.

CYNTHIA and JAN rush in.

                    CYNTHIA
          What was that all about?

                    LILY
          We were discussing the possibility
          of me joining a convent in Brazil.

                    JAN
          Hold on now, I'm the one who's
          still a virgin.

They all LAUGH.

                    JAN (CONT'D)
          But there is a problem.

                    CYNTHIA
          This new chick Marsha was trying to
          scare off some of the other new
          girls with her Mrs. Letts ghost
          stories.

                    JAN
          So I opened my big fat mouth and
          told everyone about the seance.

                    LILY
          Great! The more the merrier. Let's
          get Marsha to convince Hef.
                    (pinching Jan's cheek)
          And make sure you, our little
          virgin, gets to be the Playmate of
          the year.

                    JAN
          How can I do that if I don't sleep
          with Hef?

                    LILY
          We scare Marsha to death.

BETH, Playboy's West Coast Photo Editor enters, interrupts.

                    BETH
          Please God, no more deaths. Playboy
          Magazine is suffering enough from
          all the bad press as it is.

JAN and CYNTHIA move to exit, LILY is stopped by BETH.

                    BETH (CONT'D)
          Lily, we have decided to move
          forward and publish your centerfold
          in next year's January issue. Sort
          of a New Year's Eve special
          edition.

On Lily's reaction.

                    BETH (CONT'D)
          What's wrong dear?

                    LILY
          Well I-

                    BETH
          Don't tell me you're having second
          thoughts!

                    LILY
          It's just that-

                    BETH
          Twenty-thousand dollars. That's the
          amount we cut a check in your name,
          cashable when the clock is stroking
          midnight, January 1st.

                    LILY
               (whistles)
          That much?

                    BETH
          So let's plan some additional, what
          we call small camera shots.
          Clothed, of course. How's next
          weekend sound?

                    LILY
          Oh. Well, I and some other
          Playmates were trying to plan a
          seance.

                    BETH
          Perfect! I was stuck on ideas. I'll
          get Hef to sign off since your
          theme evolves around the late
          20's...

INT. MANSION GUEST HOUSE/GAME ROOM - NIGHT

JAN lands in seat at seance table labeled with art deco
placard that reads "Participant".

                    MARSHA
          I'm sitting there.

                    JAN
          Actually, I am.

                    MARSHA
          But I am supposed to be sitting
          there.

LILY shoves a handful of cocktail straws in front of JAN and
MARSHA. They draw straws, MARSHA wins.

                    JAN
          I'd rather be the medium anyway.

WARDROBE PERSON guides JAN to vintage clothes rack, where JAN
selects outfit marked "Beatrice Houdini".

MAKE-UP ARTIST and HAIRDRESSER finish last touches on LILY.
PHOTOGRAPHY ASSISTANT and SET DECORATOR prepare props.

LILY, JAN, MARSHA, CYNTHIA, and two other PLAYMATE SEANCE
PARTICIPANTS prepare themselves.

RICHARD SNAPS random camera shots of LILY and the others who
form a circle with hands touching.

Low filtered light reflects upon their faces from lit
candles.

JAN chants, pauses between words to read from script.

                    JAN (CONT'D)
          Rosabelle-answer-tell-pray, answer-
          look-tell-answer, answer-tell.

                    LILY
          No, no, no. You did it wrong. We
          are supposed to summon her spirt,
          and we will know if she is here if
          someone utters the code!

                         JAN
          What's the code again?

                    LILY
          Hair-pin!

                    CYNTHIA
          Shhh!

JAN's eyeballs roll back in the sockets. The table shakes.
LILY and the other three SEANCE ATTENDANTS, hold their
ground.

                    JAN
               (unearthly vocals)
          She is looking for her...

JAN points a spirit-possessed finger straight at LILY.

RICHARD SNAPS a photo of LILY's reaction.

                    JAN (CONT'D)
          ...but...no...the ebony beauty will
          soon be here, she is not among
          you...

JAN's eyelids close.

                    CYNTHIA
          That was so fucking cool! Let's do
          it again!

                    MARSHA
               (horrified)
          You guys. Look!

A TRANSLUCENT AMANDA, BLACK HAIR FLOWING, HOVERS IN THE
CORNER FOR ALL TO SEE.

                    CYNTHIA
          Who the hell is that?

                    LILY
          It's her.

PLAYMATE SEANCE PARTICIPANT

Shhh!

JAN's eyelids open, exposing only white sclera.

                    JAN
                (unearthly vocals)
           Ah- man- dah.

                  CYNTHIA
           Oh, fuck.

RICHARD enterprises on the moment. SNAP. SNAP. SNAP.

JAN passes out. MARSHA springs up from her seat, the GHOST OF
AMANDA vanishes.

                   LILY
           Where's Marsha going?

PLAYMATE SEANCE PARTICIPANT

She pissed her pants.

PHOTOGRAPHY assistant waves smelling salts underneath JAN's
nostrils.

                   JAN
           What happened?

                  CYNTHIA
           You don't remember?

LILY bites her nails.

                PHOTOGRAPHY ASSISTANT
           Not a good idea Lily.

RICHARD packs camera equipment in haste.

                  RICHARD
           I got enough, we are done here.

                   LILY
           Good. But I'm not. I need answers.

RICHARD and his PHOTOGRAPHY ASSISTANT exit as BUTLER SAM
enters. Phone RINGS.

                                        CUT TO:

EXT. PLAYBOY MANSION - IRON GATE - NIGHT

A YELLOW CAB pulls up to gate.

INT./EXT. YELLOW CAB - NIGHT

CAB DRIVER #2 rolls down window, a VOICE speaks from the ROCK
positioned on the left side of the road.

> VOICE
> (filtered)
> Name please.

DARLA, upset, in the back seat.

> DARLA
> No, no, no, no. I have a bad
> feeling.

> VOICE
> (filtered)
> Name Please.

CAB DRIVER #2

What do you want me to do lady?

The gate opens anyway!

CAB DRIVER #2

You must be special.

> DARLA
> I didn't tell anyone I was coming!

INT. PLAYBOY MANSION/GAME ROOM - NIGHT

BUTLER SAM returns phone receiver to cradle.

> LILY
> Sam, we need you to take Marsha's
> place. We want to communicate
> further with Amanda's spirit.

BUTLER SAM serves JAN a tall glass of orange juice.

> BUTLER SAM
> I'd be honored, but Hef tracked me
> down, he's requesting MAI-TAI's.
> Pronto.

EXT. PLAYBOY MANSION/CIRCULAR DRIVEWAY - NIGHT

INSIDE THE YELLOW CAB

DARLA is mesmerized by the haunting beauty of the mansion she last step foot on 50 years prior. Bittersweet.

CAB DRIVER #2

Are't you gonna get out?

A wave of guilt overcomes DARLA, frozen in time.

CAB DRIVER #2

Lady, the meter is running.

                    DARLA
          I don't like coming here one bit,
          but you see it's my granddaughter I
          got to think about. She needs me
          more than she knows.

Darla grabs her purse, squints at meter.

                    DARLA (CONT'D)
          How much do I owe ya?

INT. PLAYBOY MANSION/GAME ROOM - NIGHT

                    JAN
          Okay lets try and do this right, I
          have a series of questions to ask.
          Sort of a truth or dare game
          without the dare. Only truth. We
          want to make sure we establish a
          degree of plausibility of these
          alleged manifestations.

                    CYNTHIA
          Alleged? Oh, that's rich.

                    JAN
          Well, I never saw her.

                    LILY
          She's in my bed every night.

Everyone faces LILY with what-the-fuck expressions.

                    JAN
               (to Cynthia)
          See, told ya.

                    CYNTHIA
          Now that, my friend, I'd love to
          see.

                    LILY
          Naw. You'd best stay clear of my
          bed. Everyone I touch dies, or is
          dead already.

                    CYNTHIA
          Stop, you're making me horny.

INT. PLAYBOY MANSION/GREAT HALL - NIGHT

Front door already wide open, no one in sight, DARLA enters.
The Great Hall chandelier exudes a warm candlelight glow.

                    DARLA
          Well, I'll be damned.

Chandelier lights flicker, DARLA is drawn into flashes of
memory from that fateful night. PARTY GUESTS appear, PIANO
PLAYER, strikes keys and sings aloud to "It Had To Be You,"
composed by Isham Jones, lyrics by Gus Kahn at a piano.

Her beautiful lover AMANDA, appears at the top of the
staircase apex, in the beautiful white chiffon Channel gown
with flowing high-low hemline. AMANDA smiles. DARLA smiles.

Her raven hair now flowing, AMANDA descends the stairs as
DARLA moves trance-like toward her.

A JINGLE is heard, then a juggler's silver ball rolls slowly
toward DARLA. The sight of it hits like a dagger in her
heart, as she straddles the exact spot where AMANDA then and
now, lays dead in a pool of crimson blood, staring straight
at her.

DARLA drops to her knees, SOBS.

BUTLER DAN enters, rushes over to DARLA who is alone and
crumpled over.

                    BUTLER DAN
          M'am. Is everything all right?

DARLA raises her teary face to BUTLER DAN.

                    DARLA
          I wish to God there was a way to
          make it right. No matter what, it
          won't be right! Ever.

INT. PLAYBOY MANSION/GAME ROOM - NIGHT

Candles flutter an eerie pattern on LILY's face.

              JAN
Okay everybody, let's try and take
this serious. Lily, where do these
disturbances occur?

              LILY
Everywhere I go.

              JAN
When? How often?

              LILY
Late at night, mostly midnight.

              JAN
Does the ghost resemble a person
from the past?

              LILY   DARLA
        (simultaneous)

              YES!   YES!
All heads turn as Darla crashes the
seance prep. LILY is too stunned to
embrace Darla. DARLA is stunned at
the sight of LILY who looks exactly
like she did that night, dress,
hairstyle and all.

              DARLA
Where on earth did you get that
dress? That's my dress.

              JAN
        (addresses group)
Did you, as a witness, know about
this person, or their past.

DARLA tosses several black and white photos on the table.

              DARLA
Yes. Yes I did.

LILY inspects black and white photos, we see DARLA and AMANDA
in street clothes, arm and arm in front of a huge sign that
reads: "LDS BAPTIST OUTREACH CENTER".

              LILY
I don't understand. What's going
on?

DARLA lands at chair Marsha vacated, places her hands on
table, the others join her to create the energy circle of
hands.

                    DARLA
          Maybe she, rather, the spirit, will
          explain.

The table vibrates. JAN examines LILY.

                    JAN
          But what if she is evil-

Every single tangible item in the game room vibrates, as if
the earth was quaking. A few candles snuff themselves out.

                    CYNTHIA
          We don't need to summon her, she's
          already-

JAN's eyes roll back.

PLAYMATE SEANCE PARTICIPANT

Oh god.

JAN points a spirit-possessed finger straight at DARLA.

                    JAN
                (unearthly vocals)
          Why?

DARLA is beside herself.

                    DARLA
          I am so sorry. I have never stopped
          loving you.

Stuff flies off the walls. LILY in distress, falls face first
from chair. CYNTHIA drops to the floor, turns LILY over. LILY
foams at mouth, seizes!

JAN lets out an unearthly HOWL!

The GHOST OF AMANDA floats from corner of room, to LILY's
side, blood streams from the all orifices of AMANDA's
APPARITION, her force flings CYNTHIA across the room.

AMANDA's GHOST holds LILY in her arms.

                    DARLA (CONT'D)
          Don't touch her!

LILY snaps out of momentary catatonia.

DARLA grabs her right shoulder, GAGS, sputters, chokes, struggles to reach for her handbag.

                    LILY
               (to Amanda)
          I love you.

DARLA's handbag flies across room.

DARLA drops face first on seance table.

                    LILY (CONT'D)
          Amanda! STOP! If you love me, as
          you once loved Darla, you will
          STOP!

CYNTHIA pulls herself up off the carpet. LILY rushes to DARLA.

                    LILY (CONT'D)
               (to Cynthia)
          Cynthia toss me that handbag!

LILY checks DARLA's neck pulse.

CYNTHIA flings handbag over to LILY who retrieves and jabs insulin injector into DARLA's stomach.

AMANDA's apparition BURSTS into particles.

                                        CUT TO BLACK.

EXT. PLAYBOY MANSION/ IRON GATE - DAY

Iron gate CREAKS open.

A few BLACKBIRDS swoop down upon driveway asphalt, then waddle up toward circular driveway. LILY descends with two over-stuffed carpet bags from opposite direction, pauses a moment to glance up the rolling lawn, she shudders.

LILY tears up as she continues her descent.

In the middle of the road, a CAR idles a few feet beyond the mansion's iron gate. Lily exits, touches the large stone that houses security's speaker.

                    LILY
          Later Joe.

                    SECURITY JOE
                  (through speaker,
                   filtered)
              Take it easy my friend.

INT. CEDAR SINAI HOSPITAL ROOM - NIGHT

DARLA, hooked up to life support monitors, in bed, her chest
rises and falls to BEEP, BEEP. LILY enters, kisses DARLA on
forehead.

DARLA twitches a comatose reflex smile.

Beyond DARLA's closed eyelids we see flashes of young DARLA
and AMANDA riding bicycles, laughing, kissing.

INT. BEVERLY HILLS POLICE STATION - DAY

LILY drinks from paper cup at table, DETECTIVE SIMMS scans
folder, then closes. LILY remains poker faced.

                    DETECTIVE SIMMS
              Thanks for coming in. You know it
              was purely voluntary.

LILY darts a glance at folder pinned under DETECTIVE SIMMS's
clasped hands.

                    LILY
              Fire away.

                    DETECTIVE SIMMS
              I wanted to let you know the case
              is closed. Dirty cop with a
              reputation of false arrests and
              detainee sexual abuse has been fed
              to the fishes.

On LILY's expression.

                    DETECTIVE SIMMS (CONT'D)
              What? He was already partially
              cremated.

DETECTIVE SIMMS continues, recalling the crime.

FLASHBACK

EXT. PLAYBOY MANSION BACK YARD - NIGHT

Darkness. Firework pump SOUND heard before sky lights up
figure of COP CORY in black hooded sweatshirt and street
clothes. He teeters from cable attached to AMERICAN FLAG
pole.

COP CORY surveys HUGE CYPRESS TREE, dangerously close to
ELECTRIC FENCE WIRES. Unfortunate for him, the FLAG POLE is a
Fourth of July temporary prop, CRACKS and-

                    COP CORY
                (guttural scream)
          Ahhh!!!!!

But no-one hears as FIREWORKS EXPLODE and CRACKLE, showers of
SPARKS, then a BALL of FLAMES BURST.

                    DETECTIVE SIMMS (V.O.)
          Obviously he was hoping security
          detail would be distracted during
          the firework show.

                    END FLASHBACK

                    LILY
          And why are you telling me all
          this?

Detective sifts through open folder, LILY stiffens.

                    DETECTIVE SIMMS
          I want you to feel safe. It's my
          job, not Hugh Hefner's. COP CORY
          had quite a polaroid collection of
          you.

DETECTIVE SIMMS pushes photo over. LILY inspects the photo of
her on top of Kendel during her moment of empowered ecstasy.

LILY's brow beads up with sweat. DETECTIVE SIMMS offers
handkerchief, then pushes another photo: Kendel's body on
tray at morgue.

LILY covers her mouth in shock.

                    DETECTIVE SIMMS
          Help us give this John Doe a name.

                    LILY
                (tearfully meek)
          Kendel. What happened?

LILY's face swells with vulnerability.

                    DETECTIVE SIMMS
          A freak accident we suppose,
          witnesses say he ran in front of a
          bus. No identification was found on
          him.
                    (beat)
          Thanks for coming.

DETECTIVE SIMMS thrusts hand toward LILY's to shake.
Surprised, horrified, secretly relieved, LILY shakes
DETECTIVE SIMMS HAND, rises.

                    LILY
          The pleasure is all mine.

EXT. BEVERLY HILLS POLICE STATION - DAY

LILY exits building, stops in her tracks, hands on hips.

                    LILY
          What are you doing here?

We follow LILY's POV and see her manager PEGGY, 40s.

                    PEGGY
          I came to tell you in person.
          Remember that Odets play?

But LILY's attention is fixated across the street. SOUND of
motorcycle engine. Then MOTORCYCLE COP removes his helmet.
Waves to LILY, she shudders, thankfully a bus pulls up,
blocks her vision.

                    PEGGY (CONT'D)
          Hey! What's up with you?

Bus moves on. A CHILD behind LILY YELLS.

CHILD

DAH-DEEEEE!

CHILD waves his hand to COP. LILY CHUCKLES at her own
paranoia.

                    LILY
          Nothing, just facing my demons.

                    PEGGY
          Good! Because you got the part! But
          there is small change. There is a
          sex scene.

                    LILY
          Fine by me as long as I'm on top.

INT. PLAYBOY MANSION/GREAT HALL - NIGHT

                    CHYRON: 2015
          The infamous Playboy Mansion. From
          the decor we realize it's Hef's
          Halloween Party.

HEF, his latest GIRLFRIEND, and other PARTY GUESTS look up as
a stunt actor, TINA, 20s, teeters near the wood railing,
recreating the horrible death of "Mrs. Letts" vaudeville
style.

                                        CUT TO:

CHEERS and WHISTLES surround TINA who now lays sprawled face
up, bright red blood oozing from the back of her head into a
large crimson puddle, a ghostly image floats upward, a
holograph.

TINA jumps up from foam cushion, bows. APPLAUSE ROARS. Soaked
in blood, she looks exactly like Amanda Letts.

EXT. PLAYBOY MANSION - NIGHT

Gargoyles statues atop the gothic Tudor mansion roof offer
protection over the circular driveway, as more HALLOWEEN
PARTY GUESTS pour out of parked shuttle buses.

Several HOLOGRAPHIC entities float over the Great Lawn.

TINA ventures toward a tent whose signage boasts VICTORIAN
HORROR: FREE PORTRAITS. She wipes the last bit of red stage
makeup off her jaw.

A handsome young actor REEVE CARNEY, dressed as his 2014
Penny Dreadful Tv Series character, Victorian Era Dorian
Grey, lures in TINA still costumed as Mrs. Letts. He smiles,
pulls back entrance curtain.

INT. VICTORIAN DECORATED TENT - NIGHT

REEVE points to stool by an easel.

                    TINA
          Free of charge?

                    REEVE
          Of course. I'm really a better
          musician than painter, but I
          couldn't resist when my manager
          said I would get paid handsomely.

                    TINA
          As handsome as you, I do hope.

REEVE paints with fervor.

                    REEVE
          Complement appreciated.
               (studies Tina)
          I do say you have a rather glowing
          complexion yourself.

WEIRD AL YANKOVITCH bursts into tent dressed as a
cheerleader.

                    WEIRD AL
          Hey Reeve, hurry up, you're gonna
          miss the annual Houdini Seance in
          the Game Room!

Reeve applies finishing touches to portrait.

                    REEVE
          No can do buddy, I have a permanent
          station tonight.

TINA jumps up.

                    TINA
          I'm in!
               (to Reeve)
          Gotta go, keep the portrait for
          prosperity's sake.

TINA follows WEIRD AL through curtained exit.

                    REEVE
          Hey! What's your name?!

REEVE assesses the tent interior, reorganizes, cleans paint
brushes. BILL MAHER, dressed as Dracula, enters. BILL is
drawn to the painted portrait.

                    BILL MAHER
          Wow, you really caught the fabled
          Playboy Mansion Ghost well. How
          much?

                    REEVE
          Ghost? Sorry, it's not for sale.

BILL hands REEVE a c-note.

                    REEVE (CONT'D)
          I'll wrap it up.

EXT. VICTORIAN DECORATED TENT - NIGHT

TEN FEET TALL MONSTERS mingle with other guests on the
colorfully lit lawn. EERIE MUSIC, FAKE SCREAMS, holographic
entities float about in the full moonlit sky.

LILY dressed as Black Lilith, emotes success. She waves
goodbye to MARK and MARILOU HAMILL. BILL joins LILY, they
head back to the main house.

INT. PLAYBOY MANSION - NIGHT

At the entrance BILL coat-checks the art-work with HOSTESS
then hands LILY the ticket.

                    LILY
          Thanks. I'll store Tina's next to
          mine in the basement.
                    (on Maher's smile)
          What? I'll catch up with her later.

                    BILL MAHER
          You're such a cougar.

                    LILY
          Who says only men can date the
          younger ladies? Let's work the
          room, say our hellos to Hef.

LILY and BILL slide through CROWD in Great Hall, toward the
tented dance floor area in the Mansion's sprawling back yard.

                          THE END.

CREEPY MUSIC UNDER.

ROLL CREDITS

EXT. FORMER PLAYBOY MANSION - SUNSET - MID CREDITS SCENE

Birdseye view of grounds under massive re-construction. A
sliver of the main house remains standing.

                    CHYRON: 2021
               Across from the West Wing, next to
               turret, we focus in on two shadowy
               figures side by side.

It is AMANDA and DARLA in their 1928 New Year's Eve garb.
They clutch hands as they fade through what is left of the
front door.

                                        FADE TO BLACK.

www.ingramcontent.com/pod-product-compliance
Lightning Source LLC
Chambersburg PA
CBHW071932120726
48001CB00005B/1941